T0085556

THE CROSS OF ST. BONIFACE

BY ROBERT E. WATERS

For my mother, Nancy Waters;
thanks for letting me be weird

Cover by Jan Kostka

Zmok Books an imprint of
Winged Hussar Publishing, LLC,
1525 Hulse Road, Unit 1,
Point Pleasant, NJ 08742

This edition published in 2017

ISBN 978-1-9454300-6-0

Library of Congress No. 2017962215

Bibliographical references and index

1. Fantasy 2. Epic Fantasy 3. Action & Adventure

For more information on Winged Hussar Publishing, LLC,
visit us at: www.WingedHussarPublishing.com

Twitter: WingHusPubLLC

Facebook: Winged Hussar Publishing LLC

CONTENTS

PREFACE

March, 1501 AD, Saxony

Duke Frederick, of the Albertine line of the House of Wettin, 36th Grandmaster of the Ordo Teutonicus, and His Serene Highness, fidgeted on his throne. The smooth, dark gray tentacles that snaked out from beneath his prominent black beard always made him fidget, always brought him close to tears as he would remember again what their presence meant.

The shadowy man was near.

Duke Frederick waved his guards out of the room. When they were gone, his nefarious guest walked into the light and spoke. "You seem pensive today, Your Grace. Why do you tax your mind with such trivial concerns?"

"You consider the fate of the Order-*my* Order-the fate of the world, a trivial matter?" Duke Frederick asked, his hand shaking, the tentacles curling themselves around greasy strands of beard.

"I think you should not worry over things that you cannot control. The gods know what they are doing, and soon, all of Prussia will fall under *your* control."

"The gods? There is only one God."

The strange man leaned in close and smiled. "Are you sure?"

Suddenly, the duke's belief in one God was clouded and not so certain. Many faces invaded his thoughts, some pleasant, some devilish, some motherly, some warlike. They all fought for control of his thoughts, his beliefs, and each one seemed as legitimate as the next. He tried pushing these confusing images out of his mind, to concentrate on the one thing that gave him joy.

All of Prussia will fall under your control.

It was a tantalizing, exciting proposition. That was why, years ago, Duke Fredrick had decided to take a meeting with this man in dark robes, this man with leathery, sun-burnt skin whose fingers were as long as knives, his pate as bald as a goose egg, his tongue as sharp and as quick as a thief's. When he spoke, all problems seemed to fade away.

The duke smiled in his euphoria, then shook his head. "That can only happen if I have the cross."

"It has been found, Your Grace," the bald man said.

"Where?"

"In a city on the borders of the Ordenstadt, lying in repose, waiting."

Duke Frederick's heart sank. "Starybogow?"

"Yes, Your Grace."

Duke Frederick leaned back in his chair and sighed. A chill ran down his back as he recalled the history that the Teutonic Knights had with that cursed city. It was not a place he was looking forward to visiting again. But if the cross were there, if this aged, wise, councilor was telling the truth, then the only way to get it back was to send a Teutonic force there and-

"May I make a suggestion, Your Grace?" the man asked, as if he could read the duke's mind. "A large army may bring unwarranted attention to your cause and force King Alexander to meet you on a bloody field of battle. I've no doubt that the Ordo Teutonicus could sweep the fields of those Polish and Lithuanian cur, but now may not be the right time for such brute force. Perhaps a more-subtle-approach is warranted now. War can come later, when everything else has fallen into place."

Duke Frederick considered. The tentacles grew larger, longer, now twisting themselves around his neck and spreading over his broad chest. They engulfed a modest silver cross that lay against his sternum. Uncontrolled, chaotic images filled his mind. Then there was clarity, and he bolted upright in his chair.

"I will send one man to Starybogow," Duke Frederick said, all uncertainly gone. "My most capable and loyal brother."

The shadowy man winced. "Your Grace, I believe I know of whom you speak. He is skillful, indeed, but he is not a brother."

The duke nodded. "Not in the strict sense, no, but he is the most qualified for this kind of mission. He has served me in this capacity before and has never failed me. I trust him completely."

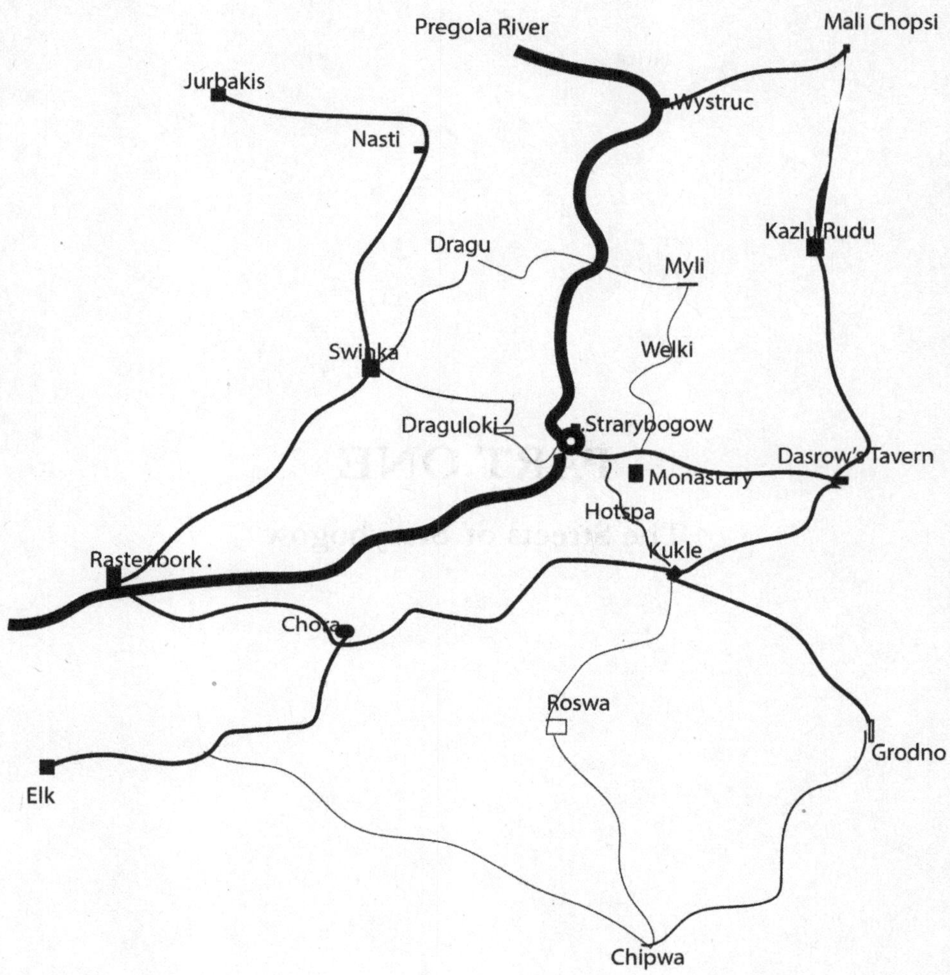

The man paused, then relented. "Very well, Your Grace. You have the wisdom of the great pharaohs."

The tentacles receded behind Duke Frederick's beard as he called for a servant. The skeletal man fell back into his shadows.

"Yes, Your Grace?" a stooped servant asked as he rushed into the room.

"Johann," Duke Frederick said, feeling like himself again. "Find Lux von Junker, and bring him to me. I, and the gods, have need of his services."

PART ONE

The Streets of Starybogow

I

The olive-skinned man in the center of the fighting pit moved like a dervish. He fought Florentine, a Turkish *kilij* sword in one hand, a Kurdish *khanjar* dagger in the other. The man facing him was a brutish oaf, big in the chest with thick, black Armenian hair covering his lacerated skin. He hacked and hammered his way forward, trying to catch the more nimble fighter by surprise, but Lux von Junker could see the exhaustion in the big man's eyes, hear the man gasping for air even from his comfortable view from the slavers' loft. The quicker man stepped aside, paused in mid-motion while the bigger fighter lost his balance. Then he struck, sliding his dagger across the nape of the man's pale broad neck with one clean stroke. The blade cut straight to the bone. The brute was dead before he hit the bloody cobbles of the fighting pit.

The crowd roared.

Lux could hardly hear himself think, let alone speak. He pointed at the victorious fighter, shouted, "Him! That's the one I want!"

"Not for sale," Stas Boyko said with a grunt.

"It's not a request, Stas," Lux said, turning to eye the old man. "You agreed to allow me my choice. I've made it. He's the one."

"I've changed my mind. He's far too valuable to free."

Lux pulled a jeweled dagger from beneath his brown robe and placed it on the table between them. "More valuable than this?" Then he reached into a loose sleeve and untied a leather bag dangling from his forearm. "Or this?"

The slaver, his eyes large with surprise, moved cautiously to the items. He ran his dry fingers over the rubies in the dagger's handle and along the blade's gold-inlaid blood groove. Then he hefted the bag, letting the enclosed gold coins click together like Spanish castanets. He smiled, forgetting himself for a moment, then grew serious again.

It was all part of a slaver's game. And Lux knew how to play that game.

"What do you want with a washed-up Tatar soldier?"

"He's a soldier?"

Stas nodded. "Was. . . or so he claims. Though he practically threw himself at me when we found him drunk, destitute, and half dead near the Pregola. He's unstable, erratic. He's got dangerous history, I'm sure."

Who doesn't? Lux turned toward the pit again and watched as the fight masters opened the gate and another poor sap lurched forward to meet his executioner.

"Regardless. I want him."

"He's Muslim, too, though I'm not sure how devout."

That paused Lux for a moment, and he considered. What would Duke Frederick say about him using a heretic on such a sensitive mission for God? Nothing, most likely, as the duke was hundreds of miles away in Saxony, and he would never know of this man if all went according to plan. In fact, no one could know why Lux von Junker was here, in Rostenbork, heading for Starybogow.

Stas Boyko huffed as if he were about to say something funny. "Judging by who you are, who you represent, I would think a Muslim in your company would bring unwarranted attention to-"

Lux brought his fist down onto the table, knocking the dagger to the floor and tossing the coins from the bag. Stas jumped, but Lux reached out fast and grabbed the slaver's silk shirt and pulled him close. "The dagger and coins are not just for that man's freedom, Stas. They're for your silence as well. You will not speak of who I am, or what I represent, or speculate among your slaver friends as to why you think I've returned. For if I find out that people are aware that I'm here, I will blame you. And then I will use that man's dagger to gut you from balls to brains." He let go of Stas's shirt. "Now. . . I will ask you once more: do we have a deal?"

The slaver fixed himself, cleared his throat, adjusted his neck, and tried to keep his anger and fear in check. "Very well. Take him."

Lux smiled and nodded politely. "May God show you mercy."

Lux turned again to the pit and watched as the fast man easily finished off his next opponent with a swift undercut of legs and a sharp jab of steel through the liver.

Lux nodded. The duke – and even God – might disapprove of his choice of partner on this mission. But the cursed city of Starybogow, looming so large down the long road that he yet had to travel, required the best, most savage fighters to survive. Lux allowed himself the small vanity that he was one of those fighters. The man in the pit, holding his bloody weapons aloft to the enraptured glee of the crowd, had already proven that he was one of them as well.

"One more thing," Lux said. "What's his name?"

*****

Fymurip Azat sat shackled in the back of his new master's wagon. It was an uncomfortable ride. It was bumpy, and the dry, cracked planks creaked back and forth as the weak, aged team stammered through the uneven ruts of the path. They were heading east; that much he could tell. And along the narrow bank of the Pregola River as well; he could smell its deep muddy flow. Where were they going? To Swinka, perhaps? Or maybe Kukle, where he had fought in another pit to the satisfaction of a bloodthirsty crowd just a few months ago. What did it matter, really? When he got there, he'd be required to kill again, and again and again, until his master's coffers swelled with coin. And perhaps this master would be generous enough to throw him a few as appreciation for a job well done. Fymurip huffed at that notion. White masters were never so generous.

He took a deep breath and laid his head back against the side of the wagon. Amid the faint light leaking through the tears in the canvas cover, he studied the crates and the few barrels packed around him. There were even a few bags of barley; for the horses no doubt, and sizable too, which meant that the man had traveled far. But there were no distinct smells in the air beyond the barley, no indication that there was anything in the crates or barrels of any merit or substance. He pushed a barrel with his sandaled foot; it moved easily. There was nothing in them. Traveling with empty containers, and east as well, where mercantile activities were scant at best. Fymurip screwed up his brow. Things weren't making sense. *Who is this man, and why is he traveling with empty crates and barrels?*

The wagon stopped, and the driver stepped off. Fymurip waited quietly as his master walked toward the back. The man opened the flaps, motioned with his left hand, and said in broken Turkish, "Come. Come on out."

He hesitated at first, his eyes adjusting to the sharp light of the setting sun. Then he crawled to the end of the wagon, letting the chains of his manacles drag along the slats.

"Please, step out."

Fymurip did as instructed, though the flay marks on his back from his last beating were growing stiff with scar tissue. He stretched his taut skin as he emerged, then straightened himself as best he could to stare into his new master's eyes. A sign of defiance; some might say, disobedience. But he was tired of looking away.

They were big, brown eyes, inset in a long, gaunt face, covered with a thin beard of graying hair. He was older than Fymurip; that was clear, perhaps twenty years or more, but the thick, loose dark robe that covered his tall frame seemed small, draped gently across his broad shoulders. He was wider than he had seemed at first. Not fat, really, but big-boned; his hands larger than Fymurip's but with fingers longer, narrower, pointy like brush needles. His nose was long and thin, and he stared at Fymurip with a wry smile on his pale lips.

He pointed to a rock at their feet. "Lay your chains over rock."

Fymurip hesitated again, then knelt and pulled his chains tight until the links were taut and straight.

Before he could look up into his master's face, the big man drew a sword and cut the chain in half.

Fymurip fell backward, his arms splayed out fully to his sides. He lay there like an image of Christ Jesus on the cross, spreading his fingers out, then making a fist, then back again. The only time in the past three years that he had ever felt this free was in the pits, killing. And now here he was, lying in the muck and mud, before a giant of a man who he thought owned him.

"I apologize that I remove your shackles cannot," the man said. "That horrid man of an excuse Boyko refused to give me key. But we'll find a way to cut them up."

Fymurip stood slowly, uncertain that he had heard the man's words correctly, his Tatar imprecise. Fymurip replied in more correct German. "You are letting me go?"

"Ah, you speak my language." The man smiled and chuckled. "And far better than I speak Tatar. Very well, then, German it is." The man reached into the back of the wagon and pulled out Fymurip's sword and dagger, cleaned and wrapped in leather. He unwrapped them and held them in the light a moment, admiring the bright glint off their newly sharpened edges, then held them out as if offering them as gifts. "Take them. They're yours. And yes, I'm letting you go. From this day forward, you are a free man, unless through careless judgment you should find your way back into Boyko's grubby hands. You may go by God's grace. But I would like to offer you an alternative path, if I may."

He offered his hand. Fymurip neither moved nor took it. The man cleared his throat, then put his hand down. "My name is Lux von Junker. I've come a long way on an important mission, and I would like you to help me complete it. Your skills as a fighter are most impressive, and I daresay that a man who can survive Stas Boyko's pits for more than three years can survive anything."

Almost anything. "Where are we going?"

Lux pointed through a tree line on the east side of the path. "Through those woods, to Starybogow."

The very word made Fymurip shudder. "It's a cursed place."

Lux nodded. "Yes, and more dangerous than any other place in the world. Or so they say; though again, I'm sure a man of your talents can survive it."

"What is your purpose there?"

"Treasure. Or, rather, one particular kind of treasure. A goblet, in fact. One that used to belong to my grandfather. He acquired it through distant relatives whose ancestors shared in Marco Polo's journey to Cathay. I never lived in the Town of the Old Gods myself, you understand, but my father would speak of it often, so much so that I can describe every jewel, every line of gold along its foot, stem, bowl, and rim. It's a priceless family heirloom. . . and I want it back."

"And you believe it has remained in Starybogow?"

Lux nodded. "When the city was ravaged by earthquakes, my father and his sister and little brother escaped. My grandfather, an old stubborn goat, refused to abandon his home. My father spoke of a tableau where he waved goodbye through gathering gray smoke as his father clutched the goblet to his breast while being consumed by the crumbling spires of St. Adalbert's Cathedral. If so, then my grandfather is buried there, his white bony hands still clutching the goblet in prayer. I want it back."

"This is all for greed."

For a moment, Fymurip thought he had erred, that taking such a confrontational tone against a man who had just cut his chains was not his best move. He had no doubt that, in a fight, he could best this tall stranger. But despite his lanky appearance, Lux von Junker was strong, and fast. He had cut those chains straight through with one swift stroke. It was not a move that Fymurip had seen often in his days as a pit fighter.

But the pale-skinned German merely paused, nodded, then continued. "One would think so, indeed. But I assure you that my reasons are pure. If anything, I wish to recover said goblet to ensure that it does not fall into the hands of a cutthroat who would exploit its value to make other lives unbearable. I do not seek to find then sell the item. I merely wish to find it and take it back home so that my family can enjoy its history."

"You have a family?"

Lux nodded. "Indeed I do. A wife, a young son, and a daughter."

"I'm surprised that you are here, then. Risking your life for such a silly thing as a cup."

"Silly to you, perhaps. But as I say, it's a part of the history of my family, and I intend on recovering it. So I ask you again. Will you help me find it?"

Fymurip fixed his sword and dagger to his belt, adjusted them so that they were equidistant from one another, the dagger on his right side and the sword on his left. He fiddled with the angle of the belt so that the sword sat a little lower on his hip. He preferred it that way; it made for a quicker draw.

He stepped forward and stared up into Lux's big eyes. "What is in it for me? You get your goblet. What do I get?"

Lux opened his palms as if in prayer. "I have already given you the greatest gift a man can give: freedom. But, if it makes you happy, you may keep all other riches that we find among those ruins. As I said, I'm not here for glory, fame, or fortune."

It was a tempting offer, indeed. Rolling images of gold coins and jewels swirled through Fymurip's mind, and it all had a favorable glow. But the man was correct. The greatest gift he had now was freedom. He had the freedom to choose, which was something he had not had for a very long time. And he was not about to let that lay fallow with indentured servitude to a man he didn't know. For that is certainly what would happen if he agreed to Lux's terms. Accepting his offer would merely replace one form of slavery with another.

Fymurip shook his head. "Thank you, sir, for my freedom. But I must decline. You may handle your own affairs as you wish, and I shall handle mine."

Lux paused, then stepped aside. He motioned to the woods. "Very well, then you may go. May God keep you safe."

Fymurip stepped carefully, afraid that it was some trick, that the man would suddenly produce another set of chains and clap them on his wrists with the same swiftness that he had cut the first set. But he reached the wood line, and nothing happened. He took a step into the wood and nothing happened. Then another and another, and suddenly he was alone. He kept walking, picking up the pace, a newfound energy in his stride. He stepped over fallen trunks, pushed through brambles, ignoring the scratches from thick needles. He brushed aside a rotten limb. He took more steps, and then the old fears returned, through the dark haze of his memory. A pair of eyes stared out at him through that haze; large, uncompromising, savage, and blood red.

Vucari eyes.

He paused, right on the lip of a ridge line, right before falling down an eroded escarpment thick with exposed roots and jagged rock. He wavered on the grassy lip, regaining his balance. He stared into the river valley below, and miles away, the ruined spires of Starybogow reached up into the clouds like broken fingers scraping a deep blue sky.

The City of the Old Gods.

He didn't even notice that Lux had come up behind him.

"She's a wondrous sight, isn't she?" Lux asked, moving to stand beside Fymurip. He pushed out a long breath, then continued. "See how the evening fog off the Pregola is drawn over the walls like a man drawing smoke from a hookah pipe, and even from this distance, you can hear the thousand sounds of those who still walk its streets. The screams, howls of the destitute, the crack of whips, the snarl of savage teeth, the clamor of steel on wood, rock against bone. Light from the setting sun casts its shadows long and deep through the detritus and filth, giving it an almost solemn, thoughtful veneer, but at its center beats a heart that God has forsaken. Scandinavians, Cossacks, Moscovites, Imperial thrill-seekers, Poles, Lithuanians, Romani and, dare I say, Tatars, all come to bask in its danger, its promise of riches and unearthly delights. Worshippers of Perun and Dazbog, Veles and Jarilo, walk its cluttered streets, sounding clarion calls for the return of the Old Gods, while Prus pagan tribesmen chitter out their foul incantations in hopes of keeping those Old Gods in dominion over the Eldar Gods. Indeed, it is not a place where humble, spiritual men like us should venture. And yet, there is no other place that I want to be. . . where I *must* be."

Fymurip turned and stared into Lux's face. "For a man that has never lived there, you sure know a lot about it."

Lux ignored the statement, turned, and said, "I know I don't have a right to ask you to help me, given your life these past few years, but I ask once more. Come with me to Starybogow and help me do God's work."

God's work? I do not worship your Christian God, German. But Fymurip did worship Allah, though he had not been given the honor these past three years of praying each day, bent on his knees to face Mecca. It would be nice to do that again. But there would be little time for that in Starybogow. Every step down its cobbled streets, its darkened alleys, would be a danger. It was madness to go down there, and yet, it was madness to be out here alone.

The red eyes of the vucari invaded his memories once more.

He turned to Lux, but instead of accepting, he pulled his *kilij* and thrust it above the German's head and into the swollen belly of a dog-sized black-and-gold spider that dangled above, readying its stinger. Lux ducked reflexively and shifted to the right, and lucky he did so, for the spider, pierced straight through, tried spraying its poison. Fymurip pulled his blade free, let the green toxic fluid squirt to the ground, then with one swift stroke, cut the spider's silk strand and let it fall to the ground. Its wounded belly popped open like a tick, and for good measure, Fymurip hacked the vile creature into three even pieces.

"God's grace!" Lux said, recovering. "What a horrid beast!"

Fymurip wiped his sword clean on nearby weeds, sheathed it, and said, "A *Pajaki* Death-Spitter. If that poison had hit your face, you would have died instantly."

"I owe you my life."

"No, sir. On that score, we are even. And yes, I will go with you to Starybogow against my better judgment. Because if I do not," Fymurip said, staring down at the gurgling pieces of the giant spider, "you will be dead in a day."

II

Lux paid a farmer six copper coins. The old man agreed to keep the wagon hidden and the team fed and well-rested. "We'll be back in a couple of days," Lux said as they readied meager provisions and fastened their blades to their belts. With a few crude chisels and a hacksaw that lay in the farmer's barn, Lux removed Fymurip's shackles. They then made for the ferry that would take them across the Pregola and up to the Konig Gate, but they would not cross until nightfall, Lux explained to Fymurip. It was a risk to cross the river by day.

"What does it matter if we wait till dark?" the Tatar asked as they entered the tree line. "You are taking us through the front door anyway."

"By night, there's little chance of being targeted by snipers or distrustful Romani from the outer wall."

"I thought you said you had never visited."

Lux shook his head. "I haven't. I've been told of the threats."

Another lie. If a cat-o-nine-tails were convenient, Lux would beat his back for the constant lying, but what choice did he have? He could no more tell this Tatar the real reason for their mission any more than he could accomplish it on his own. *I lie for God*, he kept telling himself, and it helped. *I must keep it secret until the mission is complete.*

An hour later, with the sun fully setting in the west, they stood at a guard post on the bank of the Pregola.

"No, no, no," a foul-smelling Belarus guard said with his bulky frame blocking their passage. "No one gets into Starybogow. . . especially on the ferry. It only goes north to Wystruc. It never lands on the opposite bank."

There were many Lithuanian and Belarus guardsmen strewn about the perimeter of the city with orders to keep out any thrill-seekers, vagabonds, beggars, what have you.

"But it is such a pleasant night for a river ride," Lux said, rolling a thick gold coin between the fingers of his right hand. "Be a shame to lose the chance of catching that cool breeze blowing upstream."

The guard stared down at the coin, his eyes widening. He remembered himself and cleared his throat. "There are two of you."

Lux sighed and fished into his pocket for another. He handed them over with a firm handshake. He squeezed the guard's hand a little longer, and a little stronger, than normal, making it clear that negotiations were over, and that if they persisted, the next offer would be in blood. The guard understood. He pulled away, massaged the pain out of his hand, and flipped one of the coins to a henchman.

"That could have gone badly," Fymurip whispered as they stepped onto the ferry. "You paid them too much. They will never see the likes of that coinage again. That kind of money loosens lips. They are going to talk."

Lux said nothing, but perhaps Fymurip was right. Six coppers to keep an old dirt farmer quiet was reasonable. Gold coins for a ferry ride was obscene. But he couldn't risk not getting to the other bank, couldn't waste time bargaining with foul, inconsequential guards. Now that he had gotten this far, there could be no interruptions, no further delays. He'd risk the publicity. But Fymurip did have a point.

He pulled a bag from beneath his robes and handed it over. "You are in charge of negotiations from now on."

Fymurip took the bag, stared at it through the ferryman's torchlight. It was probably more money than the Tatar had ever held in his life. He opened the bag and fished around in it, letting the gold, silver, and copper pieces tumble over each other. "This. . . this is Royal coinage. Where did you get it?"

The ferryman pushed off from the bank, and Lux shrugged. "A German nobleman traveling to Posen refused to pay my toll. I asked for it politely, but he didn't agree to the terms until I stopped twisting his neck."

Fymurip huffed. "You expect me to believe that?"

Lux pulled his robe tight against the chill off the water. He leaned forward and glared into Fymurip's eyes. "You doubt me?"

The Tatar stared for a long while, then blinked, shrugged, and turned away.

Lux relaxed and straightened, turned his head to the far bank and watched as the tiny sconces along Starybogow's high walls flicked in the wind. He closed his eyes and prayed that God would forgive him for yet another lie.

*****

No one lifts this much Royal coin from a traveler, Fymurip thought as they left the ferry behind and made it quickly up the worn escarpment toward the Konig Gate. It was an absurd statement, and perhaps a mistake by his large companion, who up to this point, had carried himself fairly well. Now, the German seemed nervous, agitated beyond comprehension. But perhaps it was not unusual. If what he said were true, getting this close to Starybogow was a milestone, and cause for concern. So close, yet so much to do to find this goblet Lux spoke of. Was there a goblet? Fymurip did not know, and in their current situation, now was not the time to press him on it.

They found the gate easy enough. The Konig entrance was a big, double-wide iron banded door that, these days, sat askance against the crumbling stone wall. One of the earthquakes that had ravaged the area had nearly torn it off its hinges. Now, it hung there on rusty joints, daring anyone to come and touch it, and risk it falling on them and smearing them into the mud and grime. They did not dare, for again, another set of guards needed tending to. These, however, were more amenable to bribery, and cost a third what Lux had paid the others. They took their money and stepped aside.

Fymurip had to admit that it was wise to enter the Konig Gate, for it was closest to the Town Hall and Igor Square. That area of the city had been decimated by quakes and years of looters. Even in the poor light of their torches, he could see the detritus and filth that had been strewn along the cobbled streets, the cluttered back alleys, and enclosed neighborhoods that lined their passage. But this part of the city was the most open, and it was far harder for any wandering brigands or cutthroats to try an ambush. Fymurip pulled both blades and kept them out and visible for anyone, or anything, that dared try a move. Lux did likewise.

The German pointed down a narrow passage through piles of broken work stones. "This way. The cathedral is near."

In its day, Saint Adalbert's Cathedral was a marvel to behold. Fymurip had never seen it without massive cracks along its base and blood-stained prayer chambers, full of rat dung and the bones of unfortunate thieves, but he had heard of its majesty upon his first arrival. The stories that the old citizenry would tell marveled any tales of Christendom and its glory days here in East Prussia. And then the earthquakes came, and then the Teutonic Knights, who slaughtered most of the citizenry in an attempt to rid the dying city of its sin and its slide back into paganism. Such an attempt had failed, of course, and now the city and its cathedral, whose ruined spires lay before Fymurip as a testament to man's infinite skullduggery, died a little death every day.

Fymurip could feel eyes upon them. Every glance left, right, behind, always seemed to flush out a streak of some shadow, some blurry mass that moved from debris pile to debris pile. Off in the distance, he could hear the howls of the ravenous, the screams of victims. There was a flush of balmy wind off the Pregola as fog drifted over the walls and settled around everything like virgin snow, and yet he felt no comfort in it. Not that he should, but behind the gray billows of condensed water, with weapons in his hands, and beside a large man wielding a massive sword of his own, Fymurip felt that he should feel more comfort, more security. He did not. It was true that every man had a destiny out there somewhere, and in this place of Old Gods, that destiny was usually a sword or a steel bolt through the heart. The difference being, most did not know when the end would come. Fymurip, however, did know his fate. *My destiny is out here somewhere*, he thought as they reached the cathedral entrance, *and it's waiting for me with teeth and claw.*

He made a move to the left toward a pathway along a line of old apartments and ruined single homes. "No," Lux said, pointing to the right and toward a dark gap between fallen columns. "Through there."

"But that will take us below the cathedral," Fymurip whispered, trying not to arouse the interest of anything watching from a distance. "Surely your grandfather's home is in this-"

"It was buried in the earthquake. It will be this way!"

It did not make any sense to Fymurip, but he let it go. He did recall Lux's comment about his grandfather being buried by falling debris, but it was very unlikely that his home would be underground. More likely the home's remains would be under piles of rock, in the direction Fymurip had suggested. *Something is not right here.*

They slipped through the gap. The way was pitch black and smelled of moldy dead things. Lux held his torch high to reveal a passage downward. Fymurip followed, keeping tight control of his blades, letting his feet fall in the exact same places as Lux's. The boards along the ground were spaced as if they were walking down stairs, but Lux's massive feet took them in stride, two at a time, as if he had been here before and knew the way instinctively. Fymurip kept close behind, letting the tall man clear the path of spider webs and dead rats that Lux kicked out of the way. He looked back over his shoulder constantly, making sure that no one followed.

Fymurip coughed. "Are you sure you know where you are going?"

"Yes," Lux said, his voice echoing through the dank tunnel. "Not much further."

The passage leveled and became wider, until it opened into a circular chamber, with three exit colonnades before them, just as dark and brooding as the passage they had entered. Lux raised his torch. What the light revealed trapped Fymurip's breath in his throat.

Stacked against the far wall were bodies, mangled and contorted into one giant mass. Limbs of half flesh, bone, and rotten wool stuck out everywhere like weeds in a field. The corpses' heads revealed damp, moldy hair of fair blonde, red, and black. The eyes inside shrunken sockets peered out in long, deadly stares, as if searching for their lost souls.

Fymurip dared take steps toward the pile, and the closer he drew to it, the more disgusted he became.

"Children! Every one of them!"

"God have mercy," Lux said, nearly dropping the torch. "They must have all died together. In the quake. A nursery, perhaps."

Fymurip found the courage to step closer and use his sword blade to push aside strands of dark hair from the sallow face of one of the victims. He leaned in and studied the exposed neck bone.

"These children did not die in the quake," he said. "Look at the deep cut on this girl's neck bone. And this one. . . and this one. No, Lux, they were murdered. Their throats cut. Probably in sacrifice to the Old Gods to keep the quakes from happening."

"Monstrous!"

Fymurip nodded. "We should bury them."

Lux shook his head. "I agree, but we don't have the time or the tools to do so. Perhaps later, when-"

His next word stuck in his throat as his eyes grew large and fearful in the shadow cast by his torch. The German was staring like a statue past Fymurip and into the pile of dead children. Fymurip dared to turn and see what Lux was staring at.

A body rose out of the pile, one of the children most certainly, and yet, this one had eyes that could see, hair prim and well-kept, with a clean white dress. It was like a spirit of one of the girls, and yet, its skin was dark and patchy. Then she changed, her dress fouled, her skin paled. From her mouth grew thin roots, from her ears fungus. She smiled a dark set of rotten teeth, opened her mouth wide, and screamed, "Baptize me!"

The shock of her voice knocked them back. The torch scattered. Fymurip held to his weapons, but tumbled backward, hitting his shoulder hard against the floor. "What is this?" He howled, trying to right himself against the waves of piercing sound flowing out of the dead girl's mouth.

"A drekavac!" Lux said, regaining control of his torch and fighting to stand.

"BAPTIZE US!!"

The ceiling was beginning to crumble. Dust and small rocks fell like rain from the cracks.

"Run!" Lux said. "Run-"

But Fymurip was already up and running, down one of the colonnades, deeper into the catacombs below the cathedral. Lux caught up quickly and they ran, together, not caring where they were headed. Fymurip knew that the only thing that mattered now was escape.

Escape from the drekavac who continued to scream as it pursued them down the tunnel, followed by an army of dead children.

III

Lux gasped for air as the dead children roiled behind him, screaming their request for baptism and reaching out with bony hands to grasp at his robes. He could not stop running, for the impetus of the unholy shamble behind him would plow him asunder, and how would he escape a pile of rotten children intent on tearing him to shreds? The key to this affair was their leader, the drekavac, which had taken the form of an undead child with bits of bone peeking through its morbid gray flesh, its eyes jaundice with yellow bile, its hair matted with dried blood and grease fat. Lux could not see the evil spirit amid the undulating pile of rotting flesh and dry bones, but if it could be brought down, then maybe. . .

"We cannot run forever," Fymurip said, a mere pace ahead of Lux. "I am tiring."

Lux was exhausted as well. The heavy clothing, the armor, the lack of sleep and food, combined with the stale, thick air of the catacombs made his lungs and flesh weaker than he realized. The Tatar was right. They had to stop, turn, and make their stand.

Lux was first, sliding to a stop across moldy damp cobbles, swinging around with his torch, and letting the flame serve as a sword. And just as he predicted, the bone pile hit them square, knocking them back against the wall of the tunnel. Lux let his torch drop. Its flame set alight several of the children, who did not seem to notice or mind that the dry stitching in their muddled clothing turned scorch black like burning leaves. They poked and scraped and gnawed at Lux's arms and legs, and the only thing that saved the big man from being eaten alive was his thick robes and armor.

He tossed them off handfuls at a time, kicking and pushing them away with but a flicker of his wrists. They were paper thin and frail, their wistful, dehydrated bodies unable to handle any significant pressure. His sword, incapable of being swung in such close quarters, served more as a hammer, and he turned it around to use its hilt as a stabbing tool, knocking child after child away with crushing blows to their ribcages.

Fymurip was faring the same, but his superior speed and sword skill allowed him to cleave heads clear off their brittle necks. His dagger was small enough to wave through the thick air and send skull after skull tumbling away.

Three bone children leapt onto the Tatar's back and began clawing at his shoulder blades. Blood was drawn, but the swift man plucked them off one by one and ended their assault by dashing them against the rock wall.

They were destroying scores upon scores of them, yet the pile never seemed to dissipate. Then Lux saw why.

Near the back of the onslaught, the drekavac waved its corporeal hands over a pile of bones. The pile would shiver and then reanimate into another deadly skeleton. The newly formed shamble would then take its place in the ranks. An endless stream of unbaptized bones to bite and claw through his mortal flesh. Seeing this, Lux realized that there was only one thing to do to put an end to this madness.

He stood and, punching a hole through the ravenous skeletons, he produced an amulet that hung from a gold chain at his neck. It had been buried beneath his robe and hauberk of chain, but now that it was free, it glowed like the Northern Star.

He held the amulet aloft as he walked toward the drekavac, and said, "Unholy spirit. . . I cast you down with this amulet of Saint George. Go now. . . and threaten the world of the living no more!"

The drekavac reared up, letting the tendrils of its undulating form swirl into a funnel. It tried to scream its dissatisfaction, baring a mouth of teeth and flicking its ghastly tongue at Lux as if it were spitting poison. "Baptize us-"

"I will do no such thing," Lux replied, holding up the amulet and letting its light bathe the entire corridor. "There are no souls left to cleanse. You have consumed them all and condemned these children to the fires of Hell. And so I say again. Leave this place!"

The drekavac tried again to resist the powerful light emanating from the amulet. It reached out to try to strike it away from Lux's hand, but the charm was too powerful, too dipped in the Word of God to destroy. It shrieked, then flew through a gap in the ceiling. It was gone, and the remaining child skeletons dropped dead to the floor.

Lux paused to ensure that the drekavac had really disappeared, sighed, then tucked the amulet away. He turned and there stood Fymurip, blades held forward, ready to strike.

"You are a Teutonic Cleric."

"Yes," Lux said. "Well, no, I am not. Not exactly. It's… complicated."

"I should have known. Your Grunwald sword, your robes, your speed and strength. I should have known that you were a warrior from the start. You lied to me."

Lux shook his head and sheathed his sword. "I freed you from your bondage. I gave you your freedom, and you made a choice."

"I would not have agreed had I known your affiliation. Teutonic Knights killed my father, a loyal servant of the sultan. They bled him out before my eyes. They raped my mother and left her for dead. *You* killed my father, raped my mother."

"*I* did these things? Or did dishonorable men, agents of the devil, do so? I cannot speak for every member of the Ordo Teutonicus. I can only speak for myself and for my lord commander, Duke Frederick. We are honorable men with an honorable purpose. I can promise you that before God."

Fymurip took a step forward. "You say that you are not a Teutonic Knight, and yet you wear the accouterments. You wield their sword. You claim Duke Frederick as your commander. How is it that you are not a knight, or, rather, it is complicated, as you say, and yet you do these things?"

Lux sighed and took a step back. He could see no reason in keeping the full truth from the Tatar now. "I was a brother in my youth. But I could not maintain my vow of chastity. I was thus removed from their service in an official capacity. I now serve them as a specialist, an honorary member, if you will, one whose skills are unique enough to forego the normal requirements of membership. And to be honest, I am greatly in Duke Frederick's favor, and so he is willing to overlook my weaknesses and bend the rules a little. As far as I'm concerned, I am a brother. Duke Frederick certainly considers me as such. I'm just not recognized as one in public."

"Very well. Now, tell me why we are really here, then! And don't lie and say it is to find a golden cup. A man who walks on unholy ground with so much gold in his purse does so under more meaningful reasons. Speak the truth, or you will lose your throat."

The Tatar placed his dagger against Lux's neck. The big man swallowed. "I doubt you have the stamina to make the slice. Step back a pace, and I will tell you."

Fymurip held his blade against Lux's neck a few seconds more, then stepped back. "Speak!"

Lux cleared his throat. "Many, many years ago, long before you and I were born, Simon von Drahe, the Grand Commander of my order, had a premonition on the night before battle. That premonition told him that he would fall against a Lithuanian and Polish force arrayed against him near the town of Dragu. So powerful was the premonition that he decided to entrust in his cleric, Gunter Sankt, with the honor of protecting the Cross of Saint Boniface."

"The Cross of Saint Boniface is a myth."

Lux shook his head. "No, my good man, it exists. Held by Christ himself before the Last Supper, he kissed it, blessed it, and imbued it with all his heavenly goodness. A pure, yet wondrous silver cross that can destroy any evil it encounters, heal even the most egregious wounds. But only in the hands of the righteous. Such a man was Saint Boniface, until he succumbed to his own mortality, where it passed from generation to generation through peace- loving hands, until it reached Commander von Drahe. But he was worried that if he fell in battle, then pagan hands would corrupt and corrode its goodness. So he gave it to Gunter the Good, who vowed upon death to keep it safe.

"The Grand Commander's premonition proved true. He fell in battle, hard, his body quartered and catapulted over the Teutonic battlements. My brothers fought bravely to avenge the death of their commander, but it was not meant to be. In the fighting withdrawal that followed, Gunter the Good fell as well, but neither his body nor the cross was ever recovered. Therein lies the legend, as you say, of Saint Boniface's cross.

"But most recently, through intelligence obtained by travelers of good character, a man has been seen walking these unholy ruins. The stories claim that he is a cleric of my order, and that he wears a cross of pure silver about his neck. And thus, I have been sent here by Duke Frederick, the lord and Grand Commander of my order, to ascertain if these travelers speak the truth. If so, I am to take this cleric back to Saxony and thus return the cross to its rightful keepers."

Fymurip huffed, but he put away his blades. "A foolish, *foolish* mission. Your cleric is most certainly dead after all these years. And the cross could be anything."

Lux nodded. "Indeed, but that is why I'm here. It's not my place to prejudge the authenticity of the stories. It is my duty to see if the stories are true."

"And if they are not?" Fymurip asked, eyeing Lux carefully, searching his face for any sign of waver or doubt. "What then? Will you kill this man whom *they* claim is a cleric. . . whoever *they* are. Will you rob him of whatever lies about his neck?" Fymurip opened his hands and swiveled in place, motioning to the naked child bones at his feet. "Look around you, Lux. This is a mere taste of what awaits you in these ruins. You go floundering around here without care or clear purpose, you will wind up dead. And that is not what I signed on to do. To find a Christian relic for an order that has brought so much pain to my people, to my family."

Fymurip seemed near tears, but Lux could see that the rage the Tatar felt kept his sorrow in check. "I am well aware of the risks in this place. That is why I asked you to help me. But we have had this conversation already, my friend. The question before you is the same as it was the moment I broke your chains. Now that you know the truth, will you still help me?"

Lux could see the uncertainty behind the Tatar's eyes. He could tell that the man wanted to say no, and yet something stayed his reply. But in the end, Fymurip shook his head.

"No. I say again, this is not what I signed up to do. I will not be party to this mad endeavor. Your mission is your own. I want no part of it."

Lux watched as Fymurip walked back down the corridor from where they had entered, picking his way gingerly through the piles of bones and tattered clothing. He wanted to call out, to try once more to convince Fymurip of the value of the mission, the righteousness of it. But he held his tongue and simply watched the man walk away.

*****

Fymurip picked a baby tooth from a bite in his forearm and let it drop to the ground. He cursed, rubbed away the pain and blood from the wound, then knelt momentarily behind a pile of stone slabs and discarded wood planks. Ahead a few hundred feet stood a group of men, talking in a circle, one pointing toward the east. Who were they? Where had they come from? What nationality? He could not discern these details through mere moonlight, for that was all he had. He had left the torch behind in the catacombs. He told himself that he had done so out of respect for Lux, despite the man's deceit. But in truth, he had just forgotten about it, so angry he was at the knight's lie. *Foolish old goat,* Fymurip thought as he waited behind the stones for the men to move on. *Floundering around in catacombs looking for a phantom.* And they had indeed found one, but not the one Lux was looking for. He'll never find what he seeks. Of that, Fymurip was certain. So what was the point of helping?

The men moved on, and Fymurip rose carefully and continued toward the Kiev Gate. He would, once and for all, leave this evil place and never return. He would go home, perhaps, or pledge his allegiance to the sultan, become once again a warrior in the Turkish ranks. Those had been good times, indeed. Why he had ever left the sultan's service he did not know. Ancient history. But what mattered now was getting to the gate and leaving Starybogow. Then he would figure out his next move.

He moved from shadow to shadow, keeping low and tight against walls and dilapidated statues that had been pushed out of Igor Square by broken crests of ground. The earthquakes had devastated this area of the city, leaving mighty crags everywhere. It was perfect for hiding, for moving stealthily, but one false step, and a person could be lost forever down one of those crags. He tucked away his sword, but he kept his dagger in hand. He needed at least one free hand to use for balance as he made his way through the debris piles. A left turn, then a right, another left, and there it lay: the Kiev Gate, its door still intact, but guarded heavily outside. It would be easy to knock on that door and request departure, but difficult to pass through it. The guards were far less accommodating when it came to letting folks out. But if need be, he'd give every coin he had to be free of this place.

The coins!

Suddenly, he remembered that he had walked away with the bag still tied to his belt. For a moment, he considered turning around and going back. But no, that would be foolish. He would not go back into those catacombs . . . *never again!*

Fymurip breathed deeply, stood straight, and took a step toward the Kiev Gate.

A massive clawed hand came out of the shadow and knocked him aside. Fymurip hit the stone hard, cried out in pain, and nearly dropped his dagger. He rolled, trying to adjust his eyes to the darkness now formed by a massive creature blocking the moon's light. He rolled again as a large, clawed foot slammed down an inch from his face. Fymurip gained his feet, slashed out with his dagger, and caught a bit of the beast's hide. But it did little damage, for an arm, roped with muscle and patches of black fur, grabbed Fymurip's shirt and hoisted him up into the air. He slashed and slashed with his dagger, but he found no hide, no meat. The beast roared and slammed him into a stone block, then pulled in close to stare into his face with red, furious eyes. The beast's rancid breath stung his lips.

"Vasile Lupu!" Fymurip managed to mumble as the vucari's malformed face snapped with bloody teeth and spit.

"You remember me," the beast said, slurring his words in broken Turkish. "I certainly remember you, Fymurip Azat. I have been waiting for you a long, long time. You are the last. You are the one who wielded the blade. You will die."

"It was not me, I swear." Fymurip tried to speak, but the vucari's hand was pressing hard on his throat. "I was ordered to do it. I. . . did not know. I. . . did not understand."

The vucari ignored his pleas and flung him aside. Fymurip soared through the air and broke his fall by stretching out his left arm and plunging into a tuft of weeds, soft mud, and ornate pebbles that lay at the base of a marble statue. The vucari pursued and tried grabbing Fymurip's leg, but was stopped cold by a bolt that struck him square in the shoulder.

The beast roared, stumbled forward, and Fymurip took this opportunity to lash out with his dagger. He swiped left to right and drove a deep cut across the beast's chest. The vucari roared again, reached up to his shoulder and broke off the bolt. Another struck him near the first, but only a glancing blow. Fymurip tried to cut the beast again, but the vucari fell back, moving to attack the person who had struck it with crossbow bolts.

That person was Lux, and though he stood on high ground overlooking the square, he could not reload his crossbow fast enough. The vucari was on him. Lux threw the crossbow aside and drew his sword, but he was only fast enough to block the beast as it lashed out with both hands, trying to maul the big man's throat.

Fymurip did not hesitate. Though weak and dizzy with pain, he drew his sword and rushed the beast, jumping a small gap in the ground and striking the vucari across the back. It was an ill-timed lunge, however, and the beast easily shrugged him off. Yet the strike distracted the vucari enough for Lux to swing his sword and lop off the left hand.

The vucari's agonized screams echoed through the ruins, and Fymurip was sure that everyone within a mile could hear it. He feared the unknown dangers the screams would bring their way. But, one crisis at a time. Lux's strike ended the fight.

Clutching the bleeding stump of his arm, the vucari jumped a large gap in the ground, turned, and roared his rage. "I will find you again, Fymurip Azat. I will find you again!"

Then it was gone, and Fymurip fell exhausted to the ground. Lux walked over to him and towered above the near impish little Tatar. "That should take care of it," he said.

Fymurip shook his head. "No conventional blade or bolt can kill it. When it is in its wolfen form, only the power of a strong talisman, or silver, can break it. I doubt that even the trinket you wear about your neck can drive away the evil in that man's body. No. Someday he will find me again, and next time, I might not be so lucky."

"Hmm!" Lux grunted, taking a seat beside him. "Seems you have been keeping secrets as well. Care to explain what that was all about?"

Fymurip hesitated, reluctant to divulge the truth. He wiped sweat from his face, stretched his back to massage away the pain running through it, and said, "I came into this area five years ago. A young, immature – dare I say, stupid – kid, fresh out of the sultan's service. I left his army because I was tired of killing for scraps, for nothing really, other than the glory of Allah. That in itself was a good reason to fight, but at the end of the day, I was weak and wanted more. Fame, glory, and gold. And Starybogow promised all of that.

"But I quickly fell in with a band of Muscovite cutthroats. I was quite surprised that they cared not that I was a Tatar of Turkish descent, and that I worshipped Allah, peace be upon Him. Like you, they cared only for my skills as a fighter, and fight I did. But soon I realized that these despicable men were not here for treasure or for glory. They were here for revenge. They just wanted to kill and rape and plunder, until every last person – Lithuanian, Polish, Cossack, you name it – who had wronged them in some way, suffered and died. I justified staying with them because we would, on occasion, enter the city and make war on those evil, horrid denizens that lurk in the shadows. . . like those dead children. That was Allah's work, I argued to myself, and so I stayed on, participating in all manner of vengeance.

"One day we were working through the ruins near The Citadel, and we caught rumor of a vucari hunting in that area, stealing little gypsy children and eating them whole. We went in and found her. But it was clear that the rumors were false. This wolf creature was just living in the area, you see, trying to survive like the rest of us. When the truth of it came to light, I tried getting them to stand down, to retreat. A vucari is nothing to trifle with, as you have seen. But they had their blood up, and nothing I could say would stay their sport. We tracked her until she was cornered. She managed to slit the throat of one of the Muscovites, but in the end, she lost her strength.

"By that time, my blood was up as well. Someone thrust a silver dagger into my hand, and I plunged it into her belly, three times. It was over, and she lay there dead. It was only afterward that we realized that she was pregnant, with two pups. We left her there on the cold marble floor and never entered the city again. But shortly thereafter, the vucari's mate, the beast you just encountered, his name being Vasile Lupu, tracked us down, one by one, and took out his vengeance. I was the sole survivor, and that is when that bastard Boyko found me. I was more than happy to be in his service, even if that meant being a slave. I wanted nothing more than to be rid of that vile creature.

"So you see, Lux. I cannot travel with you, for my curse will affix itself upon you. Wherever I go, that beast will surely follow. He waited years for me to reemerge. He will not stop this time until I am dead."

Lux listened to it all, nodding appropriately at various places. Afterward, he was silent. Then he stood, cleared his throat, and said, "I understand. But we all have our secrets, and there is no shortage of dangers lurking in these ruins. My request still stands. But if you are intent on carrying this burden on your own – a respectful decision – then I will see you to the Kiev Gate and have you on your way."

Just like that? Fymurip stared at the Teutonic Knight, not certain what to do. The man hadn't even asked for his coins back. Is he playing me? Fymurip wondered. When they reached the gate, what then? Would this man fall upon his knees and beg him to stay?

Fymurip looked deeply into Lux's eyes, trying to divine the truth. There was no malice, no deceit, no deception there. He would see Fymurip to the gate, and then happily bid him farewell.

"This cross of Saint Boniface. . . how important is it to you?"

"I have sworn an oath to the Grandmaster that I will return with it or not return at all."

"And you honestly believe that it resides somewhere within these ruins?"

Lux nodded.

Allah, forgive me for what I am about to do.

"Very well," Fymurip said, standing and turning toward Igor Square. "Follow me."

"Where to?"

"Lux von Junker," Fymurip said, not bothering to turn, "you may have Royal coin, but I am not without resources of my own. Come. We will do this *my* way."

"The cross of Saint Boniface [illegible] how important is it to you?"

IV

Just outside the little town of Draguloki, they watched the withered old man fish for carp. He had neither bait, nor pole, nor net, but he thrashed around happily in the knee-high water of the small stream that flowed a few feet from the entrance to his hovel. He would grunt and jab his hands under the water, flail around aggressively, but would always come up empty-handed. The failure didn't seem to shake his resolve. "I'm gonna get you, fishy. I'm gonna get you."

Lux shook his head. "This man is going to help us?"

"Looks are deceiving," Fymurip whispered, hoping that he was correct. It had been a long time since he had seen the hermit. He was crazy back then. Hopefully, he wasn't absolutely senile now.

Fymurip picked up a small rock and tossed it into the water near the man's legs. The splash startled the carp, and the old man fell to his knees, cursing. "Damn the gods! I nearly had it!"

"You haven't caught one since I've known you!" Fymurip said from brush cover. "Nor will you ever."

The hermit scrambled backward toward his hut. "Who is it? I warn you. . . I have strong magic."

Fymurip emerged from hiding. He smiled and put up his hand in peace. "Would you harm an old friend, Kurkiss Frieze?"

The hermit pushed strands of greasy gray hair out of his face. He squinted. "Who are you? And who is that with you?"

Lux emerged then, his hand on the pommel of his sword. Fymurip motioned toward Lux with caution. "Careful, he's not kidding about the magic."

Fymurip took a step into the water. "It is I, Fymurip Azat. Your old Muslim friend."

Kurkiss didn't seem to believe at first. He squinted again, moved forward cautiously, looked Fymurip up and down. "Impossible. He was torn to shreds by a wolf."

"Not yet," Fymurip said, lowering his hand and taking another step forward. "And I won't be until you can catch a fish with your bare hands."

Kurkiss giggled. "It's good to see you again, old friend. I had written you off." He motioned to Lux. "Who's the giant?"

Lux seemed insulted by the comment, moved his hand again to his sword. "An impatient fellow, for certain," Fymurip sighed, "and not one who can take a joke, apparently."

"No time for jokes, *my friend*," Lux said. "Daylight is wasting, and people are dying."

"Welcome to Starybogow!" Kurkiss cackled and did a little dance. "Where death is cheap and life. . . well, that's more complicated."

"Agh! We'll get nothing from this bloviating fool. Let's be off!"

Lux turned to leave, but Fymurip grabbed his arm. "Patience. Kurkiss will give us what we need."

"And what is that?" Kurkiss asked, straightening his back, though it seemed as if the weight of the world pushed down on his shoulders. The past few years had been hard on the old man, Fymurip could tell. He seemed more broken, more unsettled. Fymurip could see a tremor in the man's hand as he spoke, and he appeared to always be on the verge of collapsing. "I don't treat with Teutonic Knights."

"How did you-"

Fymurip was just as surprised as Lux at Kurkiss's statement. Nothing in the German's outward appearance gave away the truth, though the sword might have been a clue, or his height, or his arrogant impatience.

"He is a knight indeed," Fymurip said, deciding there was no reason to lie about it, "and he is on a very important mission. We need to find a man, a Teutonic cleric in fact, who has been seen in Starybogow."

Kurkiss waved off the request. "I don't travel in those ruins anymore. Bad for my arthritis."

"No, but you still know everything and everyone. Surely that hasn't changed."

Kurkiss paused, stared at them cautiously, and rubbed his chin as if he were deciding their fate. Perhaps he was. "Very well. We can talk. But he won't fit in my house."

They followed Kurkiss across the stream and into a small clearing on the left side of his hut. There, a pot of water boiled over a small fire, and dried ash stumps had been set up to use as chairs. Atop the stumps were what looked like black, shrunken heads, but on further scrutiny, were simple macramé balls affixed with button eyes and dried corn husks for hair.

"Meet the family," Kurkiss said, motioning to each as he lifted them gently and set them on the ground. "Batushka and Matushka. . . oh, and of course, my wife, Helena. They like the cool breeze of a morning and the warm flames of the fire as they await breakfast. But sit, sit. . . they are happy to give you their chairs."

Fymurip and Kurkiss sat quickly, but Lux could not find a comfortable stump. He settled on the damp ground next to Matushka.

"The gods have cursed you with so much girth," Kurkiss said, giggling at Lux's misfortune.

"There is only one God, old man, and my girth, as you call it, has served me well."

"Perhaps. But what do you do, I wonder, when hiding from mice, or from roaches, or from-"

"Kurkiss!" Fymurip snapped. "Focus, please."

The hermit shook his head as if to clear away the fog, then nodded. "Of course, of course. So, tell me whom you seek in the old city."

Fymurip laid out the mission as best as he could. Lux chimed in on occasion to fill in any missing pieces. When they were finished, Kirkiss reached down and scooped up a handful of dirt, dried leaves, and sticks, and tossed them into the boiling pot.

"An old Bosnian woman taught me this little trick. Then I found out that she was Baba Yaga and had to kill her." He chirped like a bird. "I do miss her cooking."

He swirled the dirt mixture with a wooden spoon, then let the inertia of the stir die down. Fymurip stood and gazed into the pot, watching as the boiling water sizzled and popped around the dirty pebbles. To him, the mixture had no distinctive shape, nor did it suggest anything resembling a location or a direction in which they might go. It looked like nothing more than wet dirt and leaves.

But Kurkiss gasped, stepped back from the pot, made the sign of divinity over his chest, and fell back onto an ash stump.

"What is it? What do you see?" Lux asked, rising from the ground.

"Your deaths," Kurkiss said. "Both of you. Abandon this mission. Now."

"Did you see the cleric?" Fymurip asked.

The hermit nodded. "Yes."

"Where is he?"

"I don't know. He was in motion, near The Citadel, I think. The vision was not clear. Romani surrounded him. He is being protected by them. They will kill you if you try to find him. So I say again, abandon this mission. It is not safe."

"Why do they protect him?" Lux asked. "We will do him no harm."

Kurkiss shook his head. "It isn't you that they fear. They are afraid of who else wants the cross."

"Who?" Fymurip reached out and put his hand on the hermit's frail shoulder. "Who wants it?"

Kurkiss shivered as if cold, but he stood, opened his mouth, and tried to answer. "The Han-"

Before he could finish, a shaft came out of the thicket behind his hut and struck the hermit in the neck.

Kurkiss Frieze fell dead at Fymurip's feet.

*****

Before the hermit's body hit the ground, Lux was up and setting a bolt in his crossbow. Fymurip had already reached the woods' edge in pursuit of the assassin. Lux followed closely behind, finding it difficult to negotiate the thick underbrush, the branches and sharp nettles ripping at his clothing and skin. The Tatar moved with ease, but the assassin was fast, agile, and it was clear from Lux's position that a confrontation had not occurred. Lux burst his way through the wood, crashing and plowing the brambles like a mad boar.

Finally, the bolt was ready. He raised the crossbow to his shoulder and aimed as carefully as he could as he stepped out into a small clearing. He pulled the trigger. The bolt found flesh in the assassin's hip. Lux smiled at his accuracy, until he realized that he had shot a dead man.

"He's already dead," Fymurip said. "He cut his own wrists with a poison blade."

Lux clipped the crossbow to his belt and knelt down beside the assassin's body. The poison had worked fast. Already the corpse's eyes bulged purple. His throat was puffy and red. His veins ran dark green, giving his face a striped marble appearance. His lips were bloodless.

"Nasty poison," Lux said, picking around the body, looking for clues, anything to indicate who he was, who he worked for.

"He must have been tracking us from the city," Fymurip said. "Maybe that is why it was so easy to leave."

Lux nodded. "I would say so. And clearly, he didn't want the old man to tell us why we shouldn't find Gunter Sankt."

"But why?"

Lux rolled up the corpse's sleeve and pointed at a blood-smeared tattoo. "That's why."

Fymurip leaned in and gasped when he saw it. It was a tattoo of two black birds, back to back. Both had red beaks and talons, and in the center of their bodies, lay a plain red-and- white shield. In the corner of the white part of the shield lay the capital letter H.

"The Hanseatic League."

Fymurip whispered the term as if doing so loudly was a curse itself. Lux had to admit some apprehension at uttering the name as well, for the Hanseatic League was nothing if not diabolical. Headquartered in the city of Lübeck, in the German state of Schleswig-Holstein, the League served primarily as a collection of merchant guilds. Though its mission seemed sincere – on the surface, at least – it dominated European trade by any means necessary. But its influence had fallen on tough times in the east, primarily in Poland and Russia. Why had they employed an assassin to work in Starybogow? And why did they care at all for an old cleric with a silver cross? Surely they had no clue as to its power, and even if they did, how would it benefit them?

Fymurip put words to Lux's thoughts. "Why is the Hanseatic League here?"

Lux shook his head. He laid the corpse's arm across the man's chest, said a silent prayer for the lost soul despite his anger, and stood. He looked into the woods. Are there others? He wondered. *Are they watching us now?*

"I don't know," he said. "But I suspect the reason they didn't want Kurkiss to discourage us from finding Sankt is because they too are looking for him. They haven't been able to find him, and they must think I can do a better job than they for I am Teutonic."

"Can you?"

"No, it doesn't work that way, Fymurip. I do not share any kind of spiritual connection with a member of my order simply because we worship and serve the same God. Does it work that way with you and other Muslims? I thought not. No. We have to do the leg work. We have to find Gunter Sankt by searching Starybogow. Brick by brick, building by building, if we must. And at least the old man gave us some clue as to where to start looking."

"If we go back in, Lux, we may lead the Hanseatic League right to the very thing they want most."

"Yes, and I suspect that's exactly what they intend. And we should give them what they want. We need to let this play out as it may, if we are to learn who all the principles are in this game. I owe that much to myself, to my order, and most importantly, to Duke Frederick. We need to find Gunter Sankt before the Hanseatic League finds him, or things may escalate beyond our control."

V

Realizing that they hadn't eaten in a full day, they chose to stay at Kurkiss's hut for a few moments longer to find succor and prepare for another foray into the ruins. Lux found the notion a little unsettling: ransacking a dead man's hovel for food, and over his corpse no less. But it was either that or go back into Starybogow weak of body and spirit. They had already seen what lay waiting for them in those ruins when they were at their best. Lux shuddered to imagine what it might be like if they were fatigued.

Fymurip dug a small grave for his friend and laid him to rest. Lux had no practical idea how Muslims buried the dead, nor did he particularly care. When the Tatar wasn't looking, Lux said a small prayer of his own for the old man, and then got back to the matter at hand: finding food and clean water.

Fymurip took this time to pray to Allah.

Lux imagined that it was the man's first chance to do so since his enslavement in the fighting pits, and it looked cathartic. Fymurip did not have the traditional Turkish seccade prayer rug, and for a moment, Lux wondered if the Tatar remembered in what direction Mecca lay. Then all fell into place as Fymurip found a dry-rot potato sack and spread it out in compensation, then went to his knees in the center. Lux crawled into the dilapidated hut and gave Fymurip all the time he needed.

He found a loaf of half-moldy bread, tore off the bad portion, and ate half of the good part in one massive bite. After prayers, Fymurip did the same. They also found a wineskin of bitter dark grape, but otherwise, it was drinkable. They also found a store of cured squirrel meat, which they finished off quickly. Then Lux cleaned himself in the creek while Fymurip ran his dagger across his face to eliminate the stubble which had grown there over the past few days.

Then they let out. The sun was well past its zenith, and they dared not wait any longer. They made their way through a wet and humid landscape in the shadows of Starybogow. Kurkiss's hut was very close to the ruined city, and thus sharp, foggy spires from it rose into the sky as guideposts, leading them easily back to the Konig Gate. The trip was quick and uneventful, and the guards waiting remembered them and put out their hands for coin the minute they were spotted. Still in charge of their finances, Fymurip dipped into the bag and produced a few silver coins. The guards quickly stepped aside.

The Citadel lay in the southeast corner of the city. In its day, it had served as a natural defensive position for the citizenry, a stone-fortified keep, with its tall, Constantinople tower looking out for invaders windward. It sat atop an escarpment, and atop that lay a sturdy curtain wall which had fared relatively well in the earthquakes. The main passage up the escarpment, unfortunately, had been devastated by the quakes, and was nothing more than a long, snake-like pile of stone barely navigable by anyone without a grapple hook and maddened determination. If one were bold and foolish enough to try climbing those stones, there were entry points through the wall that lay guardless, but Fymurip had a different idea.

"There's a staricase that winds up through the eastern battlement, which lies between the tower and the Kiev Gate. Few know of this entrance. The city watch would use it to move quickly from the square to the battlements if the town had ever been breeched."

"Seems like a weak point in the defense," Lux said, but then changed his mind when he actually saw its construction.

A third of the way up the staircase, Lux noticed that some of the steps were false: strong enough to support a man-sized body, but easily cracked open. Once open, it offered a clear view to the winding stairs below, and thus burning oil or other flamable substances could be tossed in the approach of any invading force. And with the stairs so narrow, once burning bodies began stacking up, it would be near impossible for armed hostiles to get up the staircase in any orderly fashion.

They reached the top, and it took Lux several minutes of driving his thick shoulder into the splintered wood of the steel-enforced door to knock it open. Too much noise, he had to admit, but Fymurip, with his slender dagger and sword, could not break the locks free. There was no other choice.

It finally gave, and they paused a moment to let the echo of the cracking door die away. Then, they moved to a small pile of marble near the base of the barracks that lined the eastern wall.

"The old man didn't give us a clue as to where in this mess to start looking," Lux said.

"He probably didn't know."

Lux nodded. "Well, we'll have to search stone by stone. Find a door, perhaps, or a passage leading down into the hill where the old structures lay."

The Citadel had been built atop centuries of older stone work. Some claimed that the structures below the keep offered miles upon miles of corridors and hidden rooms bereft of life, and yet swarmed with all manner of ghosts and other devilment. That was one of the reasons why it had been left alone by most thrill-seekers, but that was the only logical place for Gunter Sankt to be living, if he was here at all. Lux had no desire to venture into such a dark, musty netherworld. But he saw no other option.

"We could split up," Fymurip suggested, pointing across the yard to the other side of the complex. "Sweep the ruins from the ends, inward. That'll allow us to cover more ground."

Lux shook his head. "No, that isn't a good idea. It'll be dark soon, and truth be told, I'm not inclined to search these ruins without support."

"I'm indespensible now, eh?"

Lux could see a tiny smirk spreading across the Tatar's face. He huffed. "I wasn't the one who stalked off in a fury just a day ago. If you wish to work independently, be my guest. But with this sore shoulder now, I might not be so readily available to provide assistance should your wolf come howling."

"Very well," Fymurip hissed. "Let's start over there."

They searched the ruins, starting with the barracks and working their way into the center of the complex.

They moved from building to building, many of which lay in overgrown disarray. Lots of crows, ravens, larks, and other fowl had built nests throughout the cracked stonework. Lux shooed away a hawk and snatched her eggs. He tapped one open and ate the yolk right there. Fymurip did the same with a few small sparrow eggs, then snatched a snake from its perch in a stone cruck, not to eat it, but to gather its poison and spread it along the edge of his dagger. He then tossed the snake aside and resumed his search.

An hour later, as the sun began to set, Lux's foot broke through a rotten slat.

Fymurip managed to catch him before he tumbled down the hole that the slat had covered. Lux adjusted himself, knelt down, and pulled away the remaining planks.

They stared down an old dry well. Someone had placed a ladder in it that disappeared into the darkness. Lux grabbed a torch from his hip, lit it, and set it over the hole.

"That's a good thirty feet," Fymurip said, whispering so as to not allow his words to echo down the well.

Lux nodded. "I'll go first."

Fymurip held the torch until Lux was settled onto the ladder, before he handed it down. Lux moved carefully, slowly, so as to test the ladder. But it was relatively new and well- constructed, more than capable of holding the German's weight. He moved a little faster, which allowed Fymurip to clear the top of the well and pull the slats back over to cover their descent.

Nausea struck Lux's stomach like a thunder clap. "I don't feel well," he said, pausing to let his stomach adjust.

"Neither do I," Fymurip said.

Lux tried to keep moving, but every step became harder, until his eyes could no longer adjust to the poor light. The stone shaft of the well began to quake and surge, and Lux felt the yolk of the hawk egg lurch into his throat.

He dropped the torch and barely managed to hang on. "What's happening to us?"

But Fymurip clung to the ladder as if he were about to be sick. "I-I don't-I don't-"

The last thing Lux saw before falling to the bottom of the well was the blue-green etheareal face of a Blud spirit.

*****

Fymurip awoke to a white face. The face smiled as if the man possessing it were a friend, but he didn't know who it was. Certainly not Lux, for the face was very old, the man's cheeks a pasty gray with a full white beard down to his chest. Around his neck sat a rusty gorget, and from what Fymurip could discern through the dried crust in his eyes, pieces of chain mail adorned the man's shoulders and hung loose to his waist. Somehwere below that set of thick steel links lay a white leather shirt that bore a gold cross set in a red field.

Fymurip reached for his dagger, surprised to find it still affixed to his belt, but strong hands held him firm on the stone slab.

The old man raised his hands in peace. "Calm yourself, my Turkish friend. There is no need for violence here. . . not yet anyway."

"Who. . . where am I?" Fymurip glanced around the dim room. Torches burned from sconces in the walls. At least ten men-*were some women?*-stood in the shadows of the torchlight, holding curved blades, long swords, and bows. Lux lay on a wooden table nearby, unconscience.

"Kebrawlnik does his job well," the man said.

"Who?" Fymurip asked.

"The Blud spirit that aggravated your descent down the ladder. His job is to disorient, confuse, and if the moon is right, nauseate. I cannot afford to have the wrong sort enter my home."

"Who are you?"

"The man you've been seeking." He opened his arms and bowed low. "I am Gunter Sankt, knight and cleric of the Ordo Teutonicus. Welcome."

On cue, Lux began to stir as if from a deep sleep. The Romani that had held Fymurip down now took their place beside Lux, and when he finally came to, his reaction was the same. He reached for a weapon and struggled under the tight control of the Romani. It was not quite as easy to hold Lux down, his strong arms tossing one of the Romani to the floor. Gunter Sankt moved quickly, despite his age, to calm the younger man.

"Peace, my brother," he said. "There is no need for that here. I assure you, you are among friends. You have found the man you have sought these past few days."

Lux stopped struggling, and his eyes grew large. For a moment, it looked as if he were going to kneel before Gunter Sankt and pay homage, but he paused, collected himself, and said, "The cross. Where is it?"

"In good hands, under my personal protection."

"I must see it. Now!"

Gunter sighed, shook his head in disgust, then nodded to one of his Romani who quickly left the room. "The impatience of youth. I thank God every day that I am beyond it."

"Patience is indeed a virtue, my brother," Lux said, "but I am on a mission for our Grandmaster Duke Frederick, and its mandate takes precedence. Time is not a luxury I have."

Gunter did not reply. He waited until the Romani returned with a small cedar box. He took it and opened it slowly. There, in the center of a small piece of purple felt, lay a silver cross.

It was smaller than Fymurip had imagined it. He could tell by Lux's reaction that he too shared that surprise. It was simpler, more workmanlike than he had imagined as well. Not simplistic, not at all, but it could easily be mistaken for any other silver cross worn by clergy or royalty. It could fit in the palm of a hand. It looked as if, over the years, it had been tarnished and cleaned, tarnished and cleaned. In many places, Fymurip could see the markings of polish, and at one point, it had been worn as jewelry around the neck; he could see the small clasp at the top where a chain used to lay. Apparently it had not been worn like that in a long, long time for no chain existed now. And it did not possess fine jewels and gold filigree as the stories told. The only adornment it had was a small, oval-shaped ruby in the center of the crossbar, representing the blood of Christ.

"That's it?" Lux asked, letting his voice rise.

"What were you expecting?" Gunter asked. "One big enough to carry on your back?"

"Do not blaspheme, Gunter Sankt. You are in no position to make light of this. You are in violation of your oath. Why are you here? Why have you not delivered this cross back to its rightful owner, back to the Order?"

"Its rightful owner died on his own cross centuries ago. Saint Boniface, God bless his soul, was only its caretaker, until he died in Frisia. You do not know the whole story, my brother."

"Then enlighten me," Lux said, turning to face Fymurip. "Enlighten us."

Gunter closed the box and handed it back to the Romani. Then he began. "At the Last Supper, Jesus did indeed bless this cross with his kiss. But what you do not know is that at his scourging, the whip itself hit the cross and made an indentation that imbued its finery with doubt, with anger, greed, fear, all of the terrible aspects of such a brutal act. Jesus in his final moments tried to reinvigorate the cross with another kiss, but he was too weak, had lost too much blood. And thus, the cross passed from him into the wider world, where it moved from hand to hand, unclean, cursed if you will, until it reached the Ordo Teutonicus, and to Simon von Drahe, my Lord Commander.

"By sheer will and good conscience, von Drahe almost brought it back from darkness. But his premonition of his own death before the Battle of Dragu stopped the cross's revival, where it fell into my hands. . . my, unclean, unworthy hands. For years, I tried, as von Drahe had, to bring the cross back to its glory, but I could not do it. What I could do, however, was protect it, and with the help from these fine men and women around me, I have done so. I have kept it out of the hands of sinners and of evil men who would see it used for dark purposes."

Fymurip could see that Lux's head was about to explode. He'd never seen a man's eyes bulge so red.

"What are you talking about?" Lux asked, his chest rising angrily with forced breath. "How can you possibly protect it in this godforsaken place? There is evil *here*."

Gunter nodded. "Yes, there is. But I would rather it fall into the hands of those who worship the Old Gods, than to see it back in the hands of the Order, in the hands of your duke."

"Duke Frederick is a saintly man, a pious soul! You do not know him."

Gunter wagged a finger. "Oh, but I know whom he serves, and I know what they want."

"Who?"

"The Eldar Gods."

The old man tensed as if the words themselves struck pain in his heart. Lux wanted to reach out and slap Gunter's coarse face, as if doing so would somehow force the lie back into his throat.

"That's a lie! Why would Duke Frederick be in league with those dark creatures of myth? To stray from the path of God would be an irredeemable sin. I do not believe a word of it."

Gunter scoffed. "I can assure you, Lux von Junker, that I haven't risked life and limb all these years simply to keep a silver bauble out of the hands of a saintly man."

"How do you know my name?"

Gunter chuckled. "Ferrymen have loose lips, my brother. You should not have used Royal coin."

Fymurip couldn't help but smirk as Lux gave him the evil eye. But the big man recovered quickly. "Perhaps I did that on purpose. Perhaps I knew that word would get back to you that a Teutonic Knight was in town."

"Perhaps," Gunter admitted. "But now that you have found me, you refuse to believe what I say."

"Because it's ridiculous. As I've said, Duke Frederick wants the cross simply to bring it back to Saxony, so that it may lay in state as a reminder of our charge and duty to fulfill God's promise. That is all."

Gunter shook his head and moved forward. Fymurip reflexively placed his hand on his dagger, then thought better of it. The old man wasn't moving in anger, or to place hands on Lux. He was simply moving closer to whisper his next words.

"My young brother, one of the hardest of the deadly sins to avoid is greed. Greed for money, for fame, for women, for power. It could very well have been the duke's original intention to heap praise and security upon the cross, as you say. But trust me when I tell you, such humility is no longer in his heart. Duke Frederick is in contact with the Eldar Gods, and they seek the cross so that they might use it as a doorway through which to cross from their ethereal realm to ours. Imagine it: what mortal army could withstand a Teutonic Knight force with Eldar Gods in its vanguard? Why, your Duke Frederick could cut a swath of death and desolation from here to Nippon. Trust me when I tell you that this is our future. . . if we allow this cross to fall into Duke Frederick's hands."

"And what of the Hanseatic League?" Lux asked. "Why do they seek the cross?"

Gunter shook his head, sighed. "That motive is harder to divine. It's unlikely that they want it simply for its silver, for its jewel. I daresay that there isn't enough raw mineral in it to pay for a night's carnal pleasure. They may or may not know its power. I suspect that they have a buyer for it, someone who knows of its nature and wishes to do the very same thing that Duke Frederick wants. There are necromantic wizards who I'm sure would love to get their bony hands on it. It's someone who's willing to pay a God's bounty, I can tell you that. And from the League's perspective, it's simply a business endeavor, one that they're willing to kill for. It cannot fall into their hands either."

Lux jumped off the table and motioned for Fymurip to follow him. They huddled in a corner, out of earshot of the Romani. "What do you think?"

Fymurip rubbed the growing stubble on his chin and exhaled deeply. "I think he's an old, senile goat. But, he may be right."

Lux shook his head. "I can't believe that Duke Frederick is working with the Eldar Gods, a man I have loved and respected for so long. It's. . . it's not possible."

Lux turned to Gunter and said, "If what you say is true, then why did you risk exposure by letting us come here? Why not kill us beforehand and keep your location a mystery?"

"God teaches us that in the midst of life, we are in death. I am in death, Lux von Junker. I am old, tired, enfeebled. My time is over. I have done all that I can do. It is your time now."

"Mine? What do you mean?"

Gunter reached for the cross again, held it up so that the torchlight caught its simple beauty. "I pass the Cross of Saint Boniface to you, to hold and to cherish, to protect, until the end of your days."

Lux shook his head, and Fymurip grabbed the man's arm in order to keep him from moving too swiftly toward Gunter, lest his actions be misinterpreted by the armed guards nearby. "Easy, my friend."

"I'm not worthy of such a charge, Gunter Sankt. I cannot-"

"Any knight who would take the council of a Muslim Tatar as easily as you is the right man. You are a brother of God, but you have a practicality of mind and of spirit that is obvious by your demeanor, your carriage. No. You're the one."

Lux dropped slowly to the floor and sat there quietly, perhaps in prayer, for a long time. He never clasped his hands together, but Fymurip could see his mouth move as if reciting words from scripture. It surprised Fymurip that Gunter Sankt said nothing nor did he move for the entire time Lux contemplated his situation on that hard, dusty floor. Perhaps they were connected mentally in some way, worshiping together, seeking truths in the ethereal plane, where all truth resided. Fymurip remembered himself having such cathartic moments in the worship of Allah before a battle, setting his mind straight for what he was required to do.

Fymurip backed away and let his friend have the time he required.

Then Lux stood, quickly, his eyes fixed on Gunter Sankt. "They're coming, aren't they?"

The old cleric nodded. "All of them, scores, perhaps hundreds. They are gathering now in the city. They will have breached The Citadel wall by morning."

"Unless we stop them," Fymurip said, surprised at his own determination. In truth, this was hardly his fight. This was a Christian battle, between Christian forces. Why not just walk away? But was it really just that? A Christian squabble? If released onto the world, the Eldar Gods would make no distinction between

Christians, Muslims, or Pagans. They would kill anything that stood in their way. Fymurip wondered if the Hanseatic League, in their desire to sell the cross for profit – if that was indeed their motive – understood that. Probably not. Men whose minds were clouded with greed were always blind to the truth.

"Very well," Lux said. "We'll face them, and we'll do what we can to turn them back. But if there's one thing I've learned in my time as a knight, it's that sometimes, the best weapon in war is chaos."

"What do you have in mind?" Fymurip asked, his interest piqued.

"They are expecting us, the Romani, the cross." Lux placed his hand on Fymurip's shoulder, and winked. "Let's give them something that they're not expecting."

VI

Lux dragged a blade over Fymurip's exposed arm. Blood spilled from the wound. The Tatar did not wince or howl in pain, but Lux could tell he was unhappy.

"This is a foolish plan," he said. "It is madness."

Lux shook his head. "Mad times demand mad tactics. It will work. It has to work. Blood of Christ," he said, patting Saint Boniface's Cross that now hung from his neck on a cord. "Blood of Fymurip Azat."

Lux let droplets of Fymurip's blood fall on a rag, then he tied the rag around a bolt, notched it in his crossbow, and let it fly over the wall and into the morning darkness of the streets below. He tied similar rags around three other bolts, and let them fly as well, all down the wall, much to the chagrin of Fymurip, who walked along with him, wounded arms crossed, eyes filled with rage and fear. Lux ignored the silent protest, though he had to admit at least to himself, that the Tatar was right. It was a risky move, and one that might backfire. But they had no other choice. None that Lux could see, anyway.

"Gunter refuses your council of safety?"

Fymurip nodded. "He wishes to go out in a blaze of glory."

"Then he shall, praise God. Is he in place? And what about his guard?"

"They are ready and waiting for whatever will come."

Lux turned and placed his hands on Fymurip's shoulders. "Then let it come."

An hour later, it came.

An entire Hanseatic army, or so it seemed to Lux. Scores of men, dressed in dark red-and-black cloaks, pouring out of the fog of Igor Square, moving in mob form – though in unison – toward the escarpment of The Citadel. From his perch on the battlements, it was difficult to know what weapons they carried, but he figured the usual swords and bows were present. Perhaps some even had crossbows, but that was unlikely. Lux looked again down the line. Every twenty feet stood a Romani with a bow, an arrow notched, waiting. Fymurip anchored the end of the line, near the door where the spiral staircase lay.

Lux raised his arm, letting the small red rag in his hand wave in the wind. He waited, waited, until the first line of men reached the wall. Down his arm came, and the Romani pulled their bowstrings back, and let their first volley loose.

Several Hanseatics fell at the base of the wall. The moving mass paused, took shelter in the rubble, returned fire, but their shafts missed the wall or ricocheted harmlessly away. Another volley followed, continuing to pin the Romani but causing no damage. Lux knew that wouldn't last for long. Seeing the ocean of men hanging behind their bowmen skirmish line, it wouldn't be long before men were climbing the escarpment, and there was no value in wasting so many shots at such a long distance.

But Lux gave them the sign to fire again, and again, and again, until their supply of arrows ran low. Many men were falling dead to the ground below them, but not enough.

"Halt!" he said, finally. "And draw swords!"

They would come now, for Gunter and his Romani did not have enough power or resources to stage a fortified defense.

Within the hour, the Hanseatic League set grapples, and sticks of ten, twelve men worked their way up the escarpment and The Citadel wall. They were supported by bow fire, which was just frequent enough to keep the Romani hiding. On occasion, Lux would order counter fire, but it did little to stem the rising tide. A Romani even cut one of the grapples, and they watched as the line of men fell screaming into the rocks below. But they couldn't cut them all, and soon the battlements of The Citadel were swarming with Hanseatic goons.

Lux tossed aside his crossbow and drew his sword. He swung it against the hasty defense of a man who had just scaled the wall, and sliced through his face with one mighty stroke. He pushed the man over the wall, hitting other men trying to reach the top, sending them falling as well. Then three came at him, swinging maces and what looked like a paddle with iron spikes. Lux let a mace graze his arm in order to find security against a block of stone. He hesitated a second, then thrust his Grunwald into the chest of another man. The blade cut clean through the ribs, getting caught as it exited the back. Lux pulled desperately on the blade as he fended off man two with his arm. The man hammered at Lux with his nail paddle. Lux ducked, placed his boot on the stuck man's chest, and finally kicked him off. He swung up with his free blade and cleaved the paddle man's throat in two. The final threat was taken down by Romani blades.

At least a dozen Hanseatics were racing toward a small clump of men in the center of the complex. Gunter Sankt stood in the middle of that clump, short sword raised in defense. Lux jumped down the battlement and raced to the old cleric's aide.

They met in the center with a crash of steel, bone, and flesh. This group of invaders was tough, skilled fighting men, clearly mercenary types employed by the League for nefarious purposes. Lux knew immediately that Gunter had not been kidding. The Hanseatic League was in it to win, to bring them all to heel and steal the cross for themselves. Clearly these men knew that Gunter was their target, but of course he no longer held the cross.

Gunter was strong, though. He tore into his assailants as if it were his last battle. And of course it might very well be. The man seemed content with that knowledge, letting his now frail body move once more like it most assuredly had when he was young and full of hope and purpose. Lux took down another with a clean hack to the shoulder, pushed the corpse aside before it hit the ground, and then stood back to back with Gunter as the attack continued.

"Do you miss it?" Lux asked.

"Miss what?"

"Being in the field. Marching under the banners of God."

Lux could not see the old man shake his head, but he imagined it. "Never. I was never good with a blade."

"Don't take me for a fool," Lux said, ducking one sword swipe and fending off another in parry. "I know skill when I see it."

The old man grunted, but said nothing. He swung his sword, and Lux responded in kind by protecting their left flank. On and on it went, until Lux could see that the fight was all but gone from Gunter. The Romani who had protected their charge were dropping one by one. Gaps in the defense became pronounced, and Lux tried plugging the holes as best as he could, turning and twisting and carving up assailants as if they were warm bread.

Fymurip screamed. Lux reflexively took a step toward the shout, then paused.

"What are you waiting for?" Gunter asked.

"I-I can't leave you here. Not alone."

"I am not alone."

It was true. From behind them, through the shadows of the ruined keep, the Blud spirit, Kebrawlnik, reached out like azure fog and enclosed the attacking Hanseatics. The spirit twisted around them like a funnel cloud, working its way through their clothing. All but one hesitated, lowered their weapons, seemingly confused. One even bent over and vomited into the weeds. Gunter Sankt reached down and grabbed up a spear in his free hand. He moved through the confused, lethargic attackers, painting mad throats with crimson stroke after stroke. "Go," he shouted. "Go and help your friend."

Lux nodded and pushed his way through the remaining attackers.

Halfway to where Fymurip stood, Lux could see the reason for the Tatar's scream.

*****

Fymurip held the gaze of the vucari. It had bounded up the winding stone staircase, killing Hanseatics as it came, tearing them to shreds in fact, and painting the walls with red gore.

"I could smell your blood for miles," Vasile Lupu hissed, licking his wet fangs with a sharp tongue.

Lux's trap had worked. Fymurip really had no doubt that it would, assuming that the vucari was somewhere in Starybogow waiting. But now it was here, and in the light of early day, the beast seemed larger, taller, and more muscular as its violent breathing puffed out its rippled chest.

"I give you one opportunity, Vasile Lupu, to abandon your lust for my death," Fymurip said, gripping his dripping dagger and sword. "This is not a fair fight. Go, and be gone forever."

The Hanseatics turned their attention to the vucari. Since it had killed everything up the staircase, they naturally assumed the beast was working for Gunter Sankt. What fools they were, caught up in the bloodlust themselves, not realizing why the wolf man was here. Fymurip did not divest them of that belief. He stood back and let them tear into one another, but the vucari gave as good as it got. Better even, for its oversized paws hammered and scraped and clawed through the mounds of Hanseatic flesh that stepped in its way. And though it received multiple cuts, and now bled from those cuts, Fymurip knew that no amount of damage to its corrupted, evil flesh could put it down.

He screamed, like Lux had instructed, then dove into the fight.

Fymurip slashed and hacked and ducked and dove through the vucari's huge arms. Now, he was on its back, stabbing down with the *khanjar*, hoping to slow the beast enough to keep it occupied. It could not die of wounds from normal blades, Fymurip knew, but it could weaken, tire. *Just enough for. . .*

He erred and failed to duck. The vucari's paw struck him in the chest and drove him against the wall. Fymurip dropped his sword, but held firm to the dagger which now he used to deflect another paw strike. He could barely breathe, the pain in his back strong as he tried to recover. But the beast was on him again, punching and kicking. Some blows found skin and bone; others were deflected, but over and over the vucari attacked, keeping his focus on Fymurip while fending off Hanseatic men who kept trying to bring their feeble weapons to bear. The chaos of the moment was overwhelming, and Fymurip drifted back and forth between understanding what was happening around him and feeling the mist of confusion. Out of the corner of his eye, he could see the blue tint of the Blud spirit whisk its way through ranks of attackers, but where was Lux? Was he dead? The blood trickling down his face obscured his vision. *Is that him? No, there he is. . .*

Fymurip felt the vucari's claws wrap around his throat. "I'll give you one last chance," he managed to squeal through the pain. "Leave now, or face certain death."

Vasile Lupu snarled a laugh through his fangs. "I don't think so, Azat. I have waited a long, long time for this, and now I will have my vengeance."

Though he was nothing more than a blur, Lux charged forward through the press of Hanseatic men, and shouted, "By the grace of God!"

Fymurip raised his hand and caught the silver cross that Lux had thrown to him. It felt slick and cold in his hand, but firm and solid. He wrapped his weakening fingers around the crossbar, raised it above his head, then brought it down forcefully into the vucari's eye.

Only a tiny spurt of blood followed the thrust, as Vasile Lupu dropped Fymurip and fell back, clutching his wounded face, trying desperately to pull the cross from his eye; it would not budge. Then light glowed from inside the silver, a clean, white blinding light as the vucari fell and howled in agony. Fymurip shuffled backward, but kept his eyes on the tortured wolf man.

The glow now was blinding, and Fymurip raised his hands to cover his eyes. Then he heard a wet pop. He forced his eyes open and saw that the vucari was no longer fighting, that his face had grown twice its size, and then burst open at the sheer power of the silver glow. It was the most terrifying thing Fymurip had ever seen, and for a brief moment, he felt sorry for the beast.

The vucari's thick claws and hide faded away, absorbed by the wan light of the cross. His snout – what was left of it – changed too, reforming into a man's shattered face. A moment later, its entire body had reshaped itself to a naked man.

The light of the cross slowly dissipated, and then disappeared.

Everything was silent. The Hanseatic invaders were gone. The battle was over.

"Cutting it close, weren't you?" Fymurip said as Lux offered his hand. He took it and stood on weak legs, wincing at the pain shooting through his back.

"Sorry. I was otherwise detained," Lux said, putting his hand on Fymurip's shoulder. "But you look no worse for wear."

Fymurip tried to smile, but his face hurt too much. "Say that to my ribs."

They walked over to Vasile Lupu and stared down at his taut, emaciated human form. The wolf curse had ravaged the man, and now he was nothing more than a bleak corpse. "Devilish," Fymurip said, as he stepped aside to let Lux bend at the knee to retrieve the cross that now lay harmlessly at the corpse's side. "I wonder who he really was."

Lux wiped the blood off the cross and put it back around his neck. "Probably just some farmer, who took the wrong turn one day going home, who never imagined living such a cursed life, and allowing that curse to consume him, body and soul." The knight reached up and closed the man's remaining good eye, then mouthed a silent prayer.

They walked to where Gunter Sankt lay among a pile of bodies. The dead cleric was covered with stab wounds and arrow shafts.

"The cross is yours, Lux," Fymurip said. "There is no way to refuse it now."

Lux nodded. "Indeed, it is. But we won't remain here with it. Now that the Hanseatic League knows where it lays, they will never stop until they have it. We must leave at once."

"Where are we going?"

"To Saxony."

"So you intend on giving the cross to the duke?"

Lux shook his head and walked to the battlement. "No. Though I cannot in my heart believe that Duke Frederick is in favor of the Eldar Gods, it would be too risky to hand it over to him at this time. No, we go there for my family, that I may secure their safe passage to France. And then, we shall go to Constantinople."

"Why? What is there?"

"I've heard of a man, a mystic, who resides in that ancient place. If there is anyone in all the world that can tell us what Saint Boniface's cross is, and what it is capable of, it is he."

Lux turned to Fymurip and offered his hand. "Are you with me?"

For a moment, it seemed as if the Tatar would decline. Now that the vucari was dead, there was nothing to hold them together. And what purpose would it serve a Muslim anyway to venture further into Germany on a quest to ascertain the nature of an ancient Christian heirloom? But as he had done from their first meeting, Fymurip surprised him.

They locked hands. "Why not? Besides, someday, we will return to this cursed city, and you're going to need my protection."

Lux smiled. "Very well. Then let's be off, before Starybogow grows dark and comes at us once more."

Together, Lux von Junker and Fymurip Azat made their way out of The Citadel and toward the Konig Gate.

PART TWO

Exodus

I

"Papa! Papa!"

Adaliz and Albrecht rushed him at the door, and Lux had never felt anything sweeter. He was a mess, dirty and smelly from the road, but it did not matter to his children. They hugged his legs, and Lux walked the twins across the room to the flaming hearth where his wife, Rosa, waited patiently.

Her hair was tucked away beneath a blue scarf. Her slender body was hidden beneath a tan shift. Her feet were covered with worn slippers. She was the model of plainness, but to Lux, she was a vision.

She fell into his arms and hugged his neck so hard it felt like snapping. The children finally let go, but Rosa held on for life.

"I prayed to God every night that you would return to us," she whispered into his neck. "I thought Duke Frederick had sent you to your death for certain this time."

"It felt that way at times," Lux replied, slowly caressing her back, daring to let his fingers reach her smooth, round backside and linger there. He was loathe to show such adult affection in front of the children, but it had been so long, and his wife was the softest thing he had felt in months. The twins giggled.

"Come," Rosa said, finally pulling away and taking his hand, "let's get you a bath." She winked. "You stink!"

As the children played outside, Rosa bathed him in an iron tub filled with warm water that she had prepared. Lux let her pour the water over his head, let her scrape his back and arms with a hard-bristled brush until he wanted to scream. She giggled as well, and forced him to stay still while she scrubbed away months of filth. Despite her harsh treatment, Lux felt relaxed and at ease. He closed his eyes and tried to doze.

"Did you find what you were looking for?" Rosa asked as she took a washcloth and slowly worked his chest and shoulders.

Lux turned his head and looked out the window toward his children. "I don't know."

"What do you mean?"

"Not here," he said, "not now. We will speak of it later."

After the bath, they dined next to the hearth. Rosa had prepared a strong rabbit stew that Lux gobbled with vigor, much to the delight of the twins, who found his uncouth eating habits amusing. Lux finally realized his lack of manners, relented, and took up the spoon that lay near his plate. It was the best meal he had had in weeks.

Afterward, he dozed beside the fire as the sun set. It was Rosa who shook him awake and took him to their bed.

He wanted to take her like a dog, to work out his frustrations and fears on her body. To assert his manhood and to take control of something again in a world that seemed to be changing before his eyes. But she was so soft and loving, her eyes searching his face for some understanding of what had happened to him in the east. He could not betray her tenderness. He turned onto his back, let her on top, and gave *her* control.

When they were finished, they lay beside each other, Rosa's head on his shoulder. He told her everything. It was a long, complicated story, and he tried not to leave anything out. It was dangerous to be so free and open with the details; having her hear it all put her life in danger. But he had to talk about it, had to go through it all once again in his mind, to make sure that even he had not forgotten anything important.

Rosa lay there and listened to it all, unflinching. "Do you trust this man? This… Muslim?"

Lux considered and then nodded. "Yes, I do, despite my better judgment. I don't believe that a man such as him, a man of Allah, would risk his life just to turn around and deceive me."

"Gold is a dangerous lure, Lux. Gold may be his god. You say that he is a Tatar soldier, or was. You say that he was once a thrill-seeker, a sell-sword. A man does not so easily discard his former actions, his former life. You are living proof of such a man, Lux, with your continued devotion to the Order, despite not truly being a brother. He may be playing you for a fool."

Lux nodded. "Maybe, but I don't see as I have much of a choice now but to play along. The die is cast, as they say. The game will be played in one way or another."

He told her more about his travels, about the lush-though often dark and brooding- countryside of East Prussia, and how he would like to visit it again someday when things were not so dangerous, so dire. Then he changed subjects and told her about where he planned to take her and the children.

"What is in France?" Rosa asked.

"Safety," Lux said. "Or so I hope. It is certainly not safe here. We will go, quietly, in the morning, before Duke Frederick learns of my return, and with God's help, may we reach Avignon in the fortnight."

"That is a long way to travel in such a short amount of time. I pray that we can make it."

"We must. It is the only way."

Rosa sat up and cupped Lux's face with her hands. "I don't like you going east again. You have just returned, and you're leaving us once more. And on your own council, not on the duke's or anyone else's. What gives you such hubris?"

"I am the guardian of the cross now," Lux said, taking her hands and removing them from his face. He sat up beside her. "It is my duty."

"And where is this cross? Hmm? Show it to me."

Lux turned away. "I don't have it."

"Where is it then?"

"I won't tell you. I cannot, lest Duke Frederick-"

The door to their house burst open, and Three Teutonic Knights, in full armor, stormed through their bedroom door. Lux recognized them all.

Rosa ducked beneath their sheets. Lux stood proudly, fully naked, and pulled his sword from its scabbard that lay on the floor beside the bed. He held it forward, the sharp tip pointed toward the face of the first knight. "Even naked, I can slice through you whoresons with ease. Leave, at once, or your blood will douse my fire."

The three knights took a step back. They looked at each other as if they were considering a withdrawal. The first knight then stood firm, placed his hand on the pommel of his sword. "There is no need for violence, Lux von Junker. We are here to escort you to Duke Frederick. He would see you immediately."

"Is it customary now for His Serene Highness to break down doors and pull his subjects from their slumber?"

The knight bowed. "My apologies, sir, for this disruption. But the duke will broach no refusal. You must come… willingly or unwillingly."

Could I take them? Seeing them standing there, filling up his house, Lux suddenly wondered if he could indeed bring them down. One, certainly. Probably two. But all three? And what if he did? When they did not return to the duke with him in tow, he'd send scores more to investigate. It would all fall apart, then. What did the duke know? Lux wasn't sure. Perhaps nothing. But now was not the time for rash action. There would be plenty of time for that later.

Lux lowered his sword. "Very well. I will attend the Grandmaster. I serve at his pleasure."

*****

Duke Frederick watched as Brother Lux von Junker was escorted into his great chamber and placed before him. He was surprised to see his subject in only a night shirt, a pair of breeches, and simple black clogs, but then he remembered that he had ordered the knight to attend at once, and perhaps he had been dragged out of bed. How could he have been so forgetful of his own command? The duke tapped his forehead with thick, clumsy fingers, trying to recall. He was becoming so forgetful these days.

Brother Junker knelt low and stayed there, waiting.

The duke cleared his throat, finally remembering. "It is well to see you again, my brother. You appear to be in good health."

"I am, Your Grace," Lux said, "and I thank you for your invitation."

"You are always welcome in my home, Lux von Junker. But I am a little confused with your behavior. Why did you not come to me immediately upon your return and brief me of your travels?"

Lux bowed lower. "I apologize, Your Grace. But… I had to see my family, to make sure they were safe. I have been gone a long, long time."

"And why would they not be safe?" the duke asked, defensively. "They were under my protection during your absence, under the protection of your own brothers."

"Of course, Your Grace. I apologize again for my lack of faith in your service to me and my family."

Let it go! The hollow voice in the duke's mind echoed loud and insistent. He abided the order, and said, "Very well, then tell me of your travels. Did you find the cross?"

Lux stood slowly and began to lay out the details of his mission. It took a long time, and Lux was quite thorough. It was a marvelous story, one of danger and drama, and for a brief moment, Duke Frederick found himself jealous. It had been ages since he had been out in the field, traveling to far off, exotic places, doing God's good work. *Oh, to be young again, and-*

"But you have not answered my question, Brother Junker. Did you, or did you not, find the cross?"

Lux cast his eyes downward. "No, Your Grace. Saint Boniface's cross was not to be found. It is not in Starybogow. I do not believe that it exists at all anymore, truth be told. There was no evidence of it in those cursed ruins, nor any evidence that it ever existed there."

"And no ageless cleric either?" The duke stroked his thick beard to keep the gray tendrils from leeching out.

Lux shook his head. "No, Your Grace. There are no other brothers in Starybogow. Just hearsay and foolish rumor."

Duke Frederick stared deeply into Lux's eyes, trying to divine the truth of his words. Lux von Junker had a strong mind, one of the strongest that the duke had ever encountered. Neither his own intuition, nor the other-worldly perceptions of the tentacles beneath his beard, could shake the truth from Junker's mind.

"I beg your forgiveness, Lord Commander," Brother Junker said, kneeling once again, and holding his arms out as if preparing to be flogged. "I have failed you. I have failed the order. I have failed my brothers. I will gladly take whatever punishment you and God deem necessary, to cleanse my flesh of the shame of failure. Speak the penance, and I will obey."

It was tempting, indeed. *The man is lying to me.* In his bones, the duke could feel it, but feeling it and knowing the truth were two different things. He could not, in good conscience, punish a brother who had, by all evidence, served his Lord Commander and his brotherhood with distinction. Perhaps a small punishment for failing to notify His Serene Highness immediately, but otherwise…

"Rise, Brother Junker," the duke said. "I thank you for your honesty, and your service. Now, go home, in peace, and await further instructions."

Brother Junker nodded, took three steps back, then turned to leave.

"Oh," the duke said after him, "how are your wife and children?"

Brother Junker halted, turned his head, smiled. "They are fine, Your Grace. Your protection of them while I was away was above reproach."

"Very good. You must bring them around sometime. I would most like to be their host for dinner."

"We would be honored, Your Grace. Whenever it is convenient for you."

Duke Frederick watched Brother Junker leave under guard. When he was alone again, the tentacles spread out from beneath his beard and covered his chest. Day by day, they grew longer and thicker.

"He is lying," said the man in shadow from behind the duke's throne.

"I know he is lying, but there is no evidence of such. I cannot accuse a brother without evidence."

"You can and you must! We need that cross, and he knows where it is. You must incentivize his desire to tell us."

"How?"

The man emerged from the shadows and moved closer to the duke. His carriage was stooped and withered, yet he seemed strong and vibrant, as if some internal force was reinforcing his heart, his mind. His face, however, grew more wrinkled with each passing day, as if the tentacles beneath the duke's beard drew power from him. His eyes were feral and red. "He loves his wife, his children, no? Perhaps he would be more willing to speak the truth if they were taken into your care and shown the gods' wrath."

The duke's mouth fell open. "Kill them?"

The man shook his head. "No, nothing so vile as death. Not yet, anyway. But if Brother Junker could see pain on their faces, as you twist and turn their tiny fingers into knots, or if you give his wife to the pleasures of his Teutonic brothers over and over again, then perhaps he would share his secrets with us."

"You are a beast!"

"No, Your Grace. I'm a humble servant of the gods, and the gods are growing impatient. The cross does exist. He knows where it is, and we must get it from him. We either get it from him, or the gods will *take* from you. What is your choice?"

The tentacles writhed across Duke Frederick's chest. He watched them as he tried to avoid gazing into the eyes of the madman before him. He tried wresting his own thoughts and mental control from that which held him so tightly. He had tried scores of times before, to no avail. The gods, as the man called them, had the duke, and they did not mean to let go.

And I must obey.

"Yes," the duke said, "you are correct. He must tell us. I will send men to his home at once."

"No need, Your Grace," the man said, drifting back into the shadows of the room. "I will gladly take care of this matter for you. I know exactly who-what-to send."

II

Fymurip Azat peered out from beneath the gray canvas covering the dilapidated cart as it rolled through the Holsten Gate and into the Free City of Lübeck. His shoulder, and his back and knees, hurt from so much crouching and sneaking about; he'd be glad to see the end of it, but not yet. He had to wait until the driver stopped. Then the Tatar soldier would leap out of the wagon, dash into the shadows, and be gone. The driver would never know, and hopefully, if Fymurip was smart and diligent enough, no one else would know either. Especially the Hanseatic League.

His *kilij* sword and *khanjar* dagger were tucked away at his belt beneath a black cloak, its hood pulled tightly around his face. He was worried that a man of his complexion might not be overlooked in such a northerly city of Germany; then again, this was the capital of the League, and perhaps men of various ethnicities and colors might travel here from afar, to trade goods and services as necessary. But as a Muslim, Fymurip could not take that chance, could not risk being seen or caught. The cross tied around his neck and tucked into the pocket of his shirt could not fall into the wrong hands either.

Fymurip sneered as he checked to ensure Saint Boniface's cross was secure. How foolish was it to bring it to Lübeck, into the heart of the League's power? How foolish would it have been to let it go to Saxony and into the waiting hands of Duke Frederick? Neither choice was palatable, so they chose the least offensive. He and Lux knew that Duke Frederick wanted it. They weren't so sure of the League's reasons. And that was why he was here.

Lübeck was a beautiful city. Fymurip could not deny that, as he stole glances of it from his hiding place. In the rays of the setting sun, the cobbled streets and the thick red brick buildings glowed with a strength that he found quite appealing. The city itself was on an island surrounded by the River Trave. A great defensive position, he had to admit, but one that might prevent a speedy retreat for a man such as himself, looking for quick answers. The answers had to be quick. He could not afford a delay. Lux and his family would be waiting in France.

Fymurip thought about his friend and wondered about his condition. Were Lux and his family well? Had he faced Duke Frederick yet? Whatever powers possessed by the cross hanging from his neck, it did not include divine sight or augury. He could not look into its lovingly simplistic metallurgy and see the fate of his partner. But it felt as if nothing bad had happened-yet, anyway-and he had learned over the years to trust those instincts.

The cart came to a stop in front of what, to Fymurip, looked like a tavern; the old horses slowly pulling up to the curb and coming to a full halt. The driver yelled some obscenity to his team and then quickly climbed out of the cart.

Fymurip crawled his way to the back of the cart, then fell quietly onto the cobbled street, like a snake coming out of an old log, or water pouring from a ladle. His motions were quick and decisive, and before the driver reached the back of his cart and pulled away the canvas, Fymurip was gone.

His destination was the *Dom zu Lübeck*, the Lübeck Cathedral. Lux had sketched a crude layout of the city in charcoal on a piece of white cloth. Fymurip pulled that cloth out from a pocket and reviewed it. Rain and wear had damaged the depiction somewhat, but Fymurip could still make out most of the intersections, most of the main buildings that he was supposed to pass by on his way to the cathedral. Lux was certain that the man Fymurip was to find there would know about all of the League's dealings. That was the hope, anyway. Whether this man would confide that knowledge to a Muslim, Fymurip did not know, but he wasn't worried about it. Bishop Dietrich Arndes would either talk willingly or talk at the edge of a knife.

He followed the route sketched on the cloth, keeping to the shadows of the setting sun as best as possible. In such a heavily fortified city as Lübeck, it wasn't hard to do. But he did not wish to draw attention to himself, so when it was necessary to cross a street against the flow of civilians, he walked slow and deliberate, keeping to himself, his head down, and his eyes forward, his hand on the pommel of his sword beneath his cloak. Some passers-by paused and stared due to his clothing, but he did not make eye contact. He did not want them to see his face, his olive skin, and alert any guards. Were there guards? Perhaps, but Fymurip had not seen any yet, praise Allah, Peace be Upon Him.

He ducked through another alley, and there it stood, across the street, its dual spires scraping low rolling clouds. It was a marvelous structure, certainly larger than St. Adalbert's Cathedral in Starybogow, and in far better condition. There seemed to be some construction taking place near its northern approach. Some scaffolding there had been erected against a newly formed wall. There were no workers, however, at this hour, and in general, the cathedral was quiet and peaceful. It would take no time at all for Fymurip to traverse the space between and sidle up against its hard outer wall. That was the easy part. But how would he get inside?

And once inside, where would he go? Lux had not bothered to give him instructions once he reached the cathedral. Perhaps the big, lumbering knight had no knowledge of the insides of the building; probably not, but it wouldn't be as easy as knocking on the front door and bidding admittance. Then again...

He stepped at the end of the alley, looked both ways, saw no one, and started to cross the street.

He stopped cold in his tracks.

Across the way, moving from shadow to shadow like himself, was a figure. Dressed in full, loose-fitting black cloak, undershirt and pantaloons, the figure was short but sleek. The person certainly knew the lay of the land better than Fymurip, as he moved carefully along the wall, ducking low and out of the way when civilians passed by. Fymurip crouched and waited, watching the figure move skillfully along the wall, until he turned a corner and disappeared.

Fymurip followed, crossing the road and taking to those same shadows as the figure he pursued. He turned the corner and saw that the figure had moved about fifty feet away. In the waning light, it was hard to keep up, but low visibility allowed for more secrecy, and Fymurip moved boldly toward the figure. The man stopped as if he had heard something, turned to look back toward Fymurip. The Tatar kept deadly still and waited until the man crouched and rummaged through a bag at his waist.

From the bag, the figure drew a hook tied to a rope. He stood, hefted the hook in his left hand, spun it around by the rope several times, and flung it up the cathedral wall. It took three tries to set the hook on a window sill on the second level. The figure tested the strength of the rope, then collected his things, and began pulling himself upward. Fymurip watched the man work his way up the rope quickly, hand over hand. Then Fymurip's mouth dropped open.

The figure climbing the rope was not a man.

*****

"We must leave at once!"

His command was more forceful than he had planned. Lux did not want to frighten his children unnecessarily, but perhaps they needed to be, as he rummaged around their home for items to stuff into the brown satchel hanging from his shoulder. "Fetch a few pieces of clothing, nothing eloquent, a toy or two if you must, then get to the wagon."

Rosa packed silently, but Lux could tell that she had many questions. She instructed the children as to what to pack, and then she guided them outside. Lux shut the door behind him, then he paused. *This may be the last time I am ever here*, he thought, enjoying one more deep breath of German air. He had been born and raised in Saxony. There was no finer place in all the world, in his modest opinion. But what future did it hold when a corrupt Lord Commander sat at the top? How corrupt was Duke Frederick? Good question, and he did not know for sure.

Corrupt enough.

"Where are we going, Papa?" Adaliz asked as Lux pulled her along by her gentle hand to the barn where the wagon waited.

"To France," he said, grabbing her by the waist and hoisting her into the back of the wagon.

"Why?"

What should I say? "Because it's a beautiful country."

Albrecht helped himself into the wagon, and Rosa climbed onto the board, held the reins, and waited. Lux gave his children the most reassuring smile that he could, then joined his wife after placing his satchel behind him on the board.

"Are you sure this is the right thing to do?" Rosa asked, whispering into his ear as he took the reins from her and guided the team out of the barn.

He didn't have to answer her question, for three riders in full Teutonic plate armor rode into the clearing in front of their house, their horses heavy with barding. That was all the answer Rosa needed.

Lux drew the wagon to a halt and said with a wave, "Peace, my brothers, and welcome, but I and my family are going for a pleasant ride. I do not have time to-"

"Silence!" the rider in the middle barked, his voice distant, feral. "You will come with us, willingly or unwillingly. But you *will* come. Duke Frederick demands it."

"I have already seen His Serene Highness today, gentlemen. Why must I be burdened with another visit?"

"No burden, Herr von Junker, but a command." In unison, they got off of their mounts and placed their left hands upon the pommels of their swords. Their coordination had a sinister, corporeal feel to it. Lux leaned forward and tried to peer into the visor of the man in the middle. Red, inhuman eyes stared back at him.

He looked at his wife, at his children. He looked at the shield and sword lying in the back of the wagon near his satchel. "Rosa, take Adaliz and Albrecht back into the house."

"Lux, don't…" Rosa started to say.

"Your wife and children will come as well," the middle knight interrupted, drawing his sword.

When the other two drew theirs, Lux rolled backward into the wagon bed and pulled his Grunwald sword. "I'm sorry, gentlemen," he said, hopping out of the wagon and placing himself between the knights and his family who were racing for the door. "I have seen enough of the Lord Commander today. Perhaps for a lifetime. I will not be going with you anywhere, nor will my family, and if you take one step toward my door, I will kill all of you."

Now that the knights stood before him, he could tell that they were a good foot, foot and a half taller, and Lux himself was a tall man. These were not men; or, rather, they were not men anymore. No men stood this tall, so broad shouldered, at least not any men Lux had ever seen. But what were they? Lux held his sword forward and edged closer. He took a sniff. He could smell their bilious stench emanating from beneath their armor. The air was heavy with their foul odor.

They were draugars. Had to be. Undead men, reanimated to serve the nefarious purposes of, what? The duke? Some puppet master standing behind him? It was hard to know. But one thing was certain: they would never reach his house alive.

They circled him, but stood back as Lux waved his sword in their protected faces. In his time with Fymurip, he had learned a thing or two about swordplay and stage craft. Fighting wasn't just an act of forcing your mass and might upon your opponent, as was often the case on a battlefield. It was also about leverage and making your opponent expose his weaknesses, and then exploiting those weaknesses. A carefully placed slice or stab could end your opponent's will to fight fast and forever. He was outnumbered, yes, but these 'again-walkers' lacked a soul, and hopefully lacked the ability to improvise when conditions changed. That was their weakness.

One attacked, raising his large sword above his head and bringing it down in a full rush against Lux. Lux waited a dangerous moment, then tucked and rolled to the left. The knight could not adjust its motion, and its sword crashed through the bed of the wagon, splintering wood, cutting deep, and getting wedged between strips of supporting iron. The drauger tried adjusting to its position, but the team, still attached to the wagon, spooked and yanked the draugar off its feet and forward. The creature was too stupid to let go, and was dragged howling down the road.

At least one was out of the way for a while. But the other two attacked him together.

Lux raised his sword and caught the blades before they cut him in two. The strength of their attack was near impossible to thwart. Lux could feel his sword crack when the two blades struck, but it held, and he pushed them back and took a swing of his own, leveling blow after blow against the face plate of the nearest draugar. The sound of his sword striking steel sent sparks flying, but did little damage. He shifted to the right, blocking sword swings as they came, both draugar now simply doing everything they could to land a blow. But Lux was faster, could anticipate their moves, though their height gave them an inherent advantage and superior position.

He turned, twisted, cutting the backs of their arms, their legs, any flesh that was exposed. But a draugar does not possess blood like a living human, and thus, no amount of slicing and stabbing seemed to slow them. Lux's arms were growing heavy, his chest heaving with gasped air. They could spar for hours, while he was growing weaker with every move. *That* was their strength.

"What are they?" Rosa yelled at him from the door.

Lux ducked a sword, but felt the counter thrust tear at his ribs. He winced, fell back, felt the trickle of warm blood. "Draugar!"

One of them heard Rosa's voice, suddenly remembered its mission, and moved toward the house. Lux turned his sword around and drove the pommel into the back of the undead knight's knee. It fell instantly and Lux twisted his sword again and drove the blade deep into the morbid flesh. The creature howled. Lux kept twisting the blade.

Then he smelled smoke and looked toward his house. It was on fire, and smoke billowed out of the door, the windows. Then flames erupted out of the windows. "Rosa!" he screamed, dropping his sword and ducking an attack from the last standing draugar. He stumbled but kept his feet. He ran into the house and saw Rosa and his children escaping through the back door.

As she stepped out, Rosa turned and said, "Burn them!"

Of course. In the heat of the fight, he had forgotten his knowledge of the supernatural. Draugar can die again, and stay dead. Fire was the best solution.

Lux watched to ensure that his family made it out alive, then he turned and waited in the middle of his house as it burned around him. It was risky to stay there, he knew, standing in the middle of fire, but what other choice did he have? In fact, he did not fear death, so long as his family was safely away from the flames. He would gladly die here with these evil beasts if it meant Rosa and the children would live.

The first one stepped through the door and into a waft of black smoke, seemingly unaware of the rising heat of the fire. Lux stood iron-footed, unbending, his hands in fists. The creature came toward him, lifted and swung its sword. Lux backed away, let the sword strike the main beam of the house. The beam cracked, wavered in place, then collapsed, bringing the roof down upon the draugar. It howled its rage as it tried to climb out of the rubble, but Lux grabbed a burning cinder and tossed it onto the shattered roof. It didn't take long for the entire pile to burst into flame. Lux backed further away and watched as the silver-steel shine of the draugar's plate mail began to blacken with heat and soot.

Finally, the second one crawled in, its leg inoperable from Lux's sword thrust. It pulled itself across the burning floor toward Lux like a wounded animal. It was faster than imagined, the imperatives of its mission, its duty to its master, paramount in its horrid mind. Lux held his breath against the choking smoke, reached into the burning rubble for a stick of flame. He pulled it out, held it high until the crawling monster was near enough, then he thrust it into its exposed legs.

Its death screams echoed throughout the popping, swirling fire.

"Get out!" Rosa said from behind the house.

Lux turned and saw that part of the exposed frame had fallen across the back door. He allowed himself a breath, coughed, then girded all his strength. He leapt forward, putting his shoulder into the blockage. It snapped beneath his weight, then he and it tumbled out in a blast of smoke, fire, and ash.

Rosa's and Albrecht's hands were on him instantly, pulling him out of the way as the rest of the roof crumbled. The entire structure was now on fire, and Lux collected himself and stood, and watched as his home, and all its memories, burned to the ground.

Adaliz came to him and hugged his waist, her little arms trembling. He patted her head, turned to his wife, and said, "We cannot stay here. We must go."

"How?" she asked. "The wagon is ruined and gone."

Lux collected his cracked sword, and together, they looked for the wagon and horses. They found them about a quarter mile up the road. The spooked horses had driven into a ditch. The damaged wagon had tipped. The third draugar that had been dragged by the wagon was gone.

"Come," he said, "let's cut the horses free and go."

They did so, and Lux led each horse back into the road. It took a little while to calm them down for riding, but eventually, they obeyed. Adaliz climbed on with Lux; Albrecht with his mother. Lux leaned over and grabbed the reins of their horse, then kicked his own horse to gain speed.

A mile up the road, the last draugar stood in their path, unmoving, its sword held forward. Not even the strong breeze which blew across the fallow fields seemed to disrupt it.

Lux halted. "We'll cut across the field," he said, leading the horses off the road.

They galloped toward a distant hillock, fresh mud hitting them as their horse's hooves cut deep. The draugar followed, at full speed. Lux was amazed at how fast it could move in plate through muddy ground. It ran so fast that pieces of its armor began to peel away, and Lux purposefully began to slow.

"What are you doing?" Rosa called back.

Lux waved her forward. "Keep going!"

He slowed until the draugar was right behind him, close enough to reach out and touch the flank of his horse. Then Lux spurred the horse hard, back in the tender spot between the hind leg and the stomach. The horse whinnied and kicked backward, striking the draugar square in the face and chest. The draugar flew backward, its armor wrenched and dented.

Three minutes later, they were back on the road, and the draugar was gone.

Lux slowed them to a trot and allowed himself to relax. A little bit, anyway. Enough to hug his daughter close and to whisper tender words into her ear.

"Are we safe now, Papa?" she asked.

Are we? Lux looked left, right. He looked behind them. Empty space. Quiet space. It seemed as if they were, but he hadn't the heart to tell her the truth.

"Yes, my sweet," he said, stoking her hair. "We are safe."

III

Fymurip wasn't surprised that the stealthy figure was a woman. He had seen his fair share of women warriors over the years, especially those who had traveled to Starybogow for fame and fortune like the men they often traveled with. He was surprised at how small she was. Women were oftentimes shorter than men, he knew, but this was a child he was watching. Had to be. And to possess such skill with a grapple, and to pull herself up so easily… she must have been trained professionally. But by whom? And for what purpose?

He watched her work up the rope, then when she got to the top and tried to unattach the grapple, he moved up to the rope through shadow and gave it a subtle tug to dislodge it from her grip. He had done this numerous times before in the City of the Gods. To the girl, he knew, it would feel like she had just lost control and had dropped it.

It worked. The rope and grapple came down in a pile at his feet. He dodged out of view once again. He could hear her curse above, in Spanish. He recognized the language, but couldn't speak it. He waited until he was certain she had moved on, then he took the grapple and rope and tossed it like she had, until it caught on something firm. He yanked on it several times to ensure security, and then followed her up the rope.

She had closed the window, but hadn't locked it. He pushed it open slowly, looking through the faint candle light spread across the large room. It was difficult to discern details, but he had enough light to navigate well enough. He listened for voices, for chanting, for anything that might give him pause. Nothing. A quiet place on a quiet evening. They suspected nothing. Why would they? A house of God. Why would they ever imagine that a Tatar would invade their peace and quiet? Guilt spread through his mind, imagining how he might feel if a Christian were doing the same as he in a Mosque. He put those thoughts away quickly. No time for doubt or apprehension.

He climbed into the room and worked quietly across it at a crouch. There was light coming from an open door on the far end. He moved to it and knelt down to peer around the corner into a long hallway. Casks of light showed an elaborately ornate colonnade with tapestries adorning rich, Gothic arches. In full light, Fymurip imagined its beauty but scorned its ostentation. He much preferred simpler, more modest accommodations for his worship of God, as he imaged that most Christians did as well; at least the ones he had met in life. He squinted against the light and could make out a shape moving at the end of the hallway.

There she was, working her way to whatever she had come for. He followed, moving when she moved, stopping when she did. They passed by many entrances, some to the sanctuary, where a few priests could be seen huddled in prayer. She let them be, and instead kept moving down the hall until she reached winding stairs upward. She took the first few rungs. She stopped when they creaked, and Fymurip could tell that she was studying the dry wood for worn patterns. She then laid her feet on those places less worn, those giving her weight more support. They too creaked, but not all of them, and so she made her way up with little noise.

Fymurip did the same, and surprisingly his steps were even quieter. It was because of his added weight. The greater pressure compressed the wood quicker and thus made for a shorter period of settlement. He followed her up, having to keep himself from moving too fast and being discovered.

When he reached the top, she was gone, down another long hallway. Both directions seemed feasible to Fymurip. Which one had she taken? If he chose the wrong one, he'd lose precious time. So he waited there, in the dark, clearing his mind of everything but his focus on listening. He breathed slowly, not allowing anything, now even his own breath, to distract him. He waited, waited. Then a faint tincture of glass came from the right. Then another, and another. Then a faint, muffled voice, almost too small to hear; but in Starybogow, Fymurip had learned to discern many sounds at once. Knowing the difference between the whistle of a crossbow shaft buzzing toward you and the whistle of the wind could be the difference between life and death.

He moved toward the clinking glass. The closer he got to it, the stronger it became, until it was all that he heard. A door stood ajar at the end of the hall. Very little light came from the room. Perhaps a few candles burned on the other side, but otherwise, it was dark. In that darkness, a green glow emanated and the smell of sulfur was strong. Fymurip took a chance and leaned toward the door. He pushed it open two further inches, careful not to let it creak on its hinges.

Near a table across the room stood an old man in a black cassock with a scarlet fascia wrapped around his waist. Fymurip could see no other clothing, not even slippers on his feet. But the red sash clearly gave him away as a bishop, according to the information that Lux had provided for identifying clergymen.

On the table where the bishop stood lay many bottles with various colored liquids, two of them sitting over flames which blackened their bowls. In those bottles boiled green liquid, one dark, the other less so. The man lorded over them and mumbled incantations that did not sound Christian to Fymurip. The words did not sound like anything he had ever heard before. The man did not seem angry when speaking them, but anxious, nervous, as if he knew what he was saying was blasphemous, but could do nothing to stop them. In his hand, he held a piece of parchment. From this distance, Fymurip could not tell what was written on it. The image on the parchment looked more like a drawing than words, though there seemed to be some script jotted at the very top. The bishop held the parchment gently, as if it were a jewel, and he smiled as he stroked it with tender fingers from his right hand.

The bishop then plucked both bottles from the flames, delicately holding them in his left hand. In his right, he clutched the parchment. He turned and walked to the middle of the room. Fymurip watched intently, never taking his eyes off of the man. In the center, the bishop upended the bottles. The hot green liquid mixed as it splashed onto the floor. The bishop turned as he poured, making a circle around him. Once complete, he hopped out of the circle, fell to his knees, and prayed.

Green mist rose from the circle of poured liquid. Fymurip could feel the heat from it as the mist wound its way upward, toward the beveled ceiling. As he prayed, the bishop uttered nonsensical words. The mist seemed to answer each phrase in kind, shifting, undulating, until it had created a perfect column of thick green fog. The bishop's eyes widened as the fog grew. He held the parchment forward toward the green fog with trembling hands, saying over and over some ghastly phrase that certainly was not Christian or holy… at least not of this world.

Then from the fog came tentacles. Thick gray fingers of wet, slimy meat that slithered up and down the column of fog, reaching out into the room, reaching toward the parchment that the bishop still held forward.

"Take it," the bishop said. "You were right all along, my Lord."

A tentacle reached toward the parchment. Whispers from a human voice came from the fog in response. The bishop bowed his head, and that's when Fymurip saw her, the thief.

She had taken position behind the bishop's alchemical table. Fymurip pushed the door open another inch, then paused. The girl pulled a small bow from beneath her robe. She notched an arrow. She rose up and aimed it at the bishop just as the tentacle wrapped itself around a corner of the parchment.

Fymurip burst into the room. He lunged at the bishop. The arrow from the girl's bow caught the bishop in the shoulder just as Fymurip stuck him and took him down. The bishop howled as they both hit the floor. Fymurip rolled away and came up holding his dagger, ready to respond to any other attempt by the girl to kill the bishop.

"You fool!" The bishop said in agony, clutching his wounded shoulder. He tried standing. "You've ruined everything!"

A roar came from the green fog. Then the tentacle wrapped itself around the bishop's ankle. The bishop screamed and clawed the wooden floor, but the tentacle was strong.

Fymurip grabbed the bishop's hand, the one which held the parchment. He pulled and pulled against the tentacle, but it was too strong.

The girl came out from the shadows and wrapped her arms around Fymurip's waist and tugged as well, but neither of their strengths were enough to keep the bishop from being dragged into the fog.

Before he let go, Fymurip grabbed a corner of the parchment. The paper ripped in half. The bishop screamed one final blast of blasphemous words, then disappeared into the fog. A few seconds later, the fog dissipated, leaving a smelly green burn mark on the floor.

Fymurip collected himself, stood, checked to ensure the cross was in its proper place, then turned to the girl. Before he got a word out, her foot rounded on his chin.

She was strong, but not strong enough to knock him out. The strike was painful, but Fymurip rolled with her foot and came up in a daze beside her. His dagger was at her throat before she could respond.

"Nice try," he whispered into her ear, feeling dizzy, trying to keep the sensation from appearing in his voice, "but you need to practice leverage. You did not put the full weight of your body behind the blow."

"Who are you?" she asked in German through the scarf around her face, her voice calm but agitated.

"I could ask the same of you," he said.

"Why are you here?"

Fymurip huffed. "Same as you, I suppose, seeking treasure."

"That is a lie! If your intent was thievery, there were dozens of trinkets that you could have stolen along the way to this room. No, I think you are here for the same reason as I."

"Oh… and what is that reason?"

She broke free from his grasp and stepped a few paces away, carefully avoiding the green burn marks on the floor. Finally, she removed her scarf. She was, indeed, a woman.

And like Fymurip had concluded, a very young one. Perhaps fifteen, sixteen years old. But there was a seriousness to her face, an aged determination that he had never seen on a woman's face before. Her hair was lighter than he had imagined, with bright strands of red accentuating deeper hues. She held her hair back from her face with a cord. Her face was smooth and round. It did not look like she could even smile, or ever had, but perhaps in her line of work, joy was not desirable. Her eyes were wide and blue.

She sniffled. "You seek the cross; or, rather, you seek those who know of it."

Fymurip's heart leapt into his throat. He fought the urge to reach for his chest to ensure it was still there, for surely they were speaking of the same cross. She didn't know it hung from his neck, and he intended to keep it that way.

"And I might have succeeded," Fymurip said, "had you not tried to kill the man."

She snarled. "My target was the creature, you fool! Had you not gotten in the way, it would be dead, Bishop Arndes would be alive, and-"

"That arrow?" Fymurip interrupted. "It wouldn't have killed anything that large, especially those tentacles."

The girl shook her head. "The poison on the tip would have done the job in good time. And I say again, if you hadn't interfered, the bishop would be explaining to me the content of that parchment."

Fymurip had nearly forgotten about it. He drew the parchment up close to his face. He could smell the green sulfuric burn marks at its edges. In the margins were scribbled indecipherable words. In its center, a partially curved outline of some kind of device or tool or board. But the image was ruined by the tear. He held only half the paper. The rest had gone through the portal with the bishop.

"Who are you?" Fymurip asked.

She sighed, shook her head. "I am Catherine. My father is King Ferdinand of Aragon. My mother, Queen Isabella of Castile."

"You are Spanish?"

Catherine nodded. "And you are perceptive."

He did not know if that was a sincere compliment or sarcasm. "You are an awfully young girl to be out here all alone in Germany, so far from home, doing whatever it is you are doing."

She seemed annoyed by his patronizing tone. "I am my own person, thank you, and I will never go back. I will not be betrothed to anyone, especially some royal fool who wishes to use me just to breed heirs. I serve myself."

"And who else?" Fymurip asked. "Surely you are not here on your own. You have a master. Who, or what, is it?"

Catherine sighed again. He could see that she was reluctant to reveal her client. "I… I serve the Hanseatic League."

"As an assassin?"

She shook her head. "No, as a specialist. I do what needs to be done. Now, your turn. Who are you? Why are you here?"

He told her as much as he was willing to say. Perhaps she knew more about who he was then she let on. If so, he was not about to help her confirm suspicions. If she worked for the League, then she might already know of the events in Starybogow. She must know of the League's attack against The Citadel. It was possible, too, that word of a Teutonic Knight and a Tatar soldier fighting on Gunter Sankt's side had reached the ears of her employer. But how much did she really know?

"So you serve Benedictine monks who wish to know the truth of Saint Boniface's cross? You, a Tatar soldier?"

Fymurip nodded and hoped it looked sincere enough. "I am not a devout Muslim, if that is what you are asking. I serve the highest number of coins. They would like to find it and keep it out of the hands of more, nefarious, interests. Do you know such interests?"

Catherine stirred and averted her eyes with that last statement. Fymurip chose not to pursue the matter for now. Instead, he raised the parchment again. "Do you know what this is?"

Catherine dared approach him. He let her, and they stared down at the wrinkled image and foreign words. "No," she said, "but maybe Georg does."

"Who is Georg?"

She did not answer. Instead, his question was followed by fearful voices and shuffling feet outside the door. "Come," she said, grabbing his arm and pulling him to a window. "We must leave now."

"Where are we going?"

Catherine gave the room's one ornate window a shove. A cool breeze flowed through and caught Fymurip in the face. It was quite refreshing. He did not realize just how hot and sweaty he had become dealing with this young, impertinent, but very skilled, woman. She climbed onto the sill, turned, and said, "Keep up, and don't look down. I don't want Tatar guts all over this pretty city."

So she does have a sense of humor. Then Fymurip looked down, and perhaps she wasn't kidding. One slip and he'd be nothing but mush on the cobbles below.

As other clergy burst into Bishop Arndes's room and gasped at the vile green stain on the floor, Fymurip and Catherine slipped through the window and disappeared into the darkness, jumping from roof to roof. Fymurip fought to keep up and made a point never to look down.

IV

They traveled for many days, stopping only long enough for quick food and water. Their flight had been so sudden and desperate that Lux had not had the opportunity to bring with him the accouterments of knighthood, those Teutonic symbols that would be recognized across Germany and respected. It was a blessing and a curse, in truth. He had his cross hanging from his neck and his Grunwald sword-damaged as it was-and felt confident in its integrity if something afoul came their way, despite the crack running up the blood groove. Lacking further evidence of his exalted status made their passing through small towns less eventful, and perhaps that was best, for if Duke Frederick had his minions in chase, lacking those symbols meant safety. Yet their absence meant that their physical privations went generally ignored by the townsfolk that they passed. As far as the citizenry was concerned, they were nothing but a poor family riding meek horses.

Lux was doing fine. He had had years in the saddle as a soldier, and experience like that hardens a man's constitution, toughens his skin and spine. Such speedy and rigorous travel was easy for a man like him. His children, however, and his wife, were not so conditioned, and after three days of the dirt and dust of the road, they grew weak and weary of the saddle, being doubled-up with their mother and father for so long. Adaliz cried whenever the ride got bumpy, her young, tender thighs having developed blisters. They stopped whenever they could, and Rosa would tend to their children's sore skin and would usually give them her portions of food to help keep their strength up.

"You cannot go without eating," Lux told her as they stopped by a creek for water and rest. "It does them no good if their mother passes out from lack of food and dehydration."

"We need to stop, Lux," Rosa said, leaning into the creek and washing clean two scarves she had been using to help soothe Adaliz's blisters. "We need a roof over our heads for one night, a warm bed and good food. It will destroy me-destroy you-if we have to bury our daughter because her blisters grow foul and feverish. They are leaking already. Next they will smell. How bad does it have to get before you will stop?"

He caught himself before snapping at her. He wanted to tell her of the drekavac and the horde of dead children that he and Fymurip had to fight off in the catacombs beneath Saint Adalbert's Cathedral. He wanted to tell her of the deep, red eyes inset into the terrifying face of the werewolf that nearly killed them both. He wanted to shout at her, *Blisters will heal, woman! I'm fighting for her mortal soul… for all of our souls. Do you not remember the draugar I just killed? There are far worse things in the world, Rosa, then a few blisters!* But he did not speak his frustrations, for in truth, she was correct. Not about Adaliz's blisters, per se. Lux had seen far worse wounds on battlefields heal within days. Adaliz was just young and tired and scared, and because of that, she was incapable of girding her courage and bearing her pain on her own. So her mother had taken up the task of giving voice to her daughter's dissatisfaction. Adaliz was in pain, yes, but she would survive. The horses, however, were another matter.

They were dying. Lux had ridden enough of them in his day to know when they were near collapse. He had pushed them too far, too aggressively. They could not keep this pace up for much longer, despite being sturdy beasts. They needed days of casual grazing and rest, days they did not have. They wouldn't last another two.

"Let us reach France," he said, taking his wife and pulling her close. "One more day, and then we will stop for a night. I promise."

Crossing the border into France was absolutely necessary, for Lux doubted that Duke Frederick would dare disrupt the sovereignty of a neighboring country by sending men across in pursuit. Then again, perhaps he would. Why would a border matter to a man under the thrall of an unknowable evil? Lux hugged his wife tightly and prayed to heaven.

They switched passengers. Albrecht rode with Lux, and Adaliz with her mother, who cradled her like a babe, keeping her thighs wrapped in scarves. Lux was worried that any slight jar might toss the girl from Rosa's arms, but she held her firm, and the girl slept as they continued their journey.

In the afternoon of the next day, they crossed the border into France and rode into the city of Strasbourg. There, a dozen armed men wrapped in the colors and symbols of the Hanseatic League were waiting.

*****

She was hard to follow, but Fymurip kept pace better than even he could have imagined. It is one thing to move swiftly through territory that one is familiar with; quite another when the ground is foreign and filled with unknown obstacles. But he watched her footfalls as best as possible in the faint moonlight. He had the fortune of having a longer stride than she, and so it took less effort to bound from one critical point to another. When she slowed to navigate a larger gap between rooftops, he was able to catch up. Only once during their flight did he pause for an extended length of time. He paused, considered his situation, tucked his shirt back in, and then caught up.

Several minutes later, they were stepping through a window and into an attic room filled with candles and bearded men.

Seven men to be exact, surrounding a large round table filled with documents and maps and books and used quills. The men themselves were dressed richly, in flowing red and violet robes, frilled golden collars, felt bonnets and hats, tan breeches, new leather boots. There was a smell of cologne in the air, and it was clear to Fymurip that these men were wealthy. These men were merchants.

These men represented the Hanseatic League.

One greeted Catherine with warmth, kissing her gently on both cheeks and then sharing a generous smile. "Catherine," he said, his voice low and husky. "It is good to see you well and unharmed."

"And you also, Georg," she said.

They paused to share in mutual admiration, and then the man turned toward Fymurip, his expression now serious. "And who is this?"

"His name is Fymurip Azat," Catherine said. "He is a Tatar, who claims to be seeking the cross for Benedictine monks."

"I can speak for myself, thank you."

"Then speak," Georg roared, as if he were announcing an act in a circus tent. "Tell us all why Fymurip the Tatar seeks a Christian artifact in the city of Lübeck."

Fymurip cleared his throat, collected his thoughts to get his story straight. "It is as she says. My employer seeks the cross, so that it may be resurrected, or destroyed."

Geog huffed. "Your employer is a fool, then. Its powers are beyond resurrection, and one wonders if it can even be destroyed. But you seek what we seek, and so come to the table, and let us discuss it." He turned back to Catherine. "Your mission failed?"

Catherine lowered her head, showing contrition. "Bishop Arndes was taken by an Eldar beast through the portal."

"Damn!" Georg's eyes grew large and terrified. "How did this happen?"

"Because..." she paused, and Fymurip stared at her as she searched for words. She diverted her eyes from his gaze, then said, "...because I missed my target."

"Did you learn *anything*?"

Catherine nodded. "I have this." She pulled the parchment from her sleeve and handed it to Georg. He unraveled it and laid it on the table. The merchants gathered around leaned in to have a look. They shook their heads. It was as puzzling to them as it was to Fymurip.

"Well," Georg said, sighing and shaking his head, "I suppose we should be thankful. It is more than we had before, though it tells me little. What do you think, Tatar?"

Fymurip stepped up to the table hesitantly. It seemed a bit odd how willing they were to trust him and ask for his opinion, but the members of the Hanseatic League must have believed time was of the essence and he cleared the doubts from his mind. Fymurip looked at the parchment once again, but in truth, his eyes looked beyond the spot of paper and studied the maps that the merchants had laid out on the table. "It is a mystery to me as well. It is certainly not an image of the cross itself."

"How do you know?" Georg asked. "Have you seen it?"

"I-I have heard a description of it, and there is nothing in those curved markings that suggest a cross. Perhaps an outline of a building, or a monument or symbol of some kind."

The merchants looked at each other. Georg studied their reaction as if he were measuring their thoughts. Catherine had come up to the table as well, but she kept her thoughts hidden. If she was trying to figure out what the image was, based on Fymurip's speculation, she did not show it. Her expression was empty. She just stared at the maps.

Georg pushed the parchment aside, then waved his hand over the table. "What do these maps tell you, Tatar?"

"My name is Fymurip," he said, growing weary of being referred to in that manner. "I am not all that familiar with Europe, but judging from the names of the towns and rivers, we are looking at Germany and France. Perhaps Spain as well?"

Georg nodded. He pointed to a circle that had been scribbled by a quill around the word 'Saxony'. "There lies the power of the Ordo Teutonicus. There lies the throne of Duke Frederick. He seeks the cross as well. Did you know that? And do you know why?"

Fymurip shrugged. "It is no concern to me. My employers do not have contact with the duke or his knights."

"How do you know that?" Catherine asked.

They waited for an answer. Fymurip did not give them one. He didn't know what to say. Finally, Georg broke the silence. "Do you know the purpose of the Hanseatic League, Tar-Fymurip? Do you know what god we serve? We serve commerce. But we also serve a greater purpose, one that few know about, but one that is absolutely necessary for the survival of the world and its institutions. Duke Frederick has been compromised by the Eldar Gods. We do not know who is pulling his strings, but we know that he seeks the cross… and he seeks what is contained on this parchment. If he gets them both, the world will fall into death and desolation. We seek to keep that from happening. You doubt me?"

Fymurip fought to keep his doubt from showing on his face. "Georg, or whoever you are, I have seen a lot of troubling things in my life. And you may be right about Duke Frederick-it is not my concern. But I have never once met a merchant who does not have his own interests at heart. I think you desire the cross so that you may keep Duke Frederick from closing or dominating the trade routes to the East."

The moment he said that, Fymurip realized he had made a mistake. But he could not take it back. All fell silent in the room, and Georg stared him straight in the eyes. He smiled, then said, "Take him!"

They moved against him faster than any merchants he had ever seen. Each had stored a dagger beneath his clothing, and they were out and moving to seize him. Fymurip turned toward the window, but Catherine barred his way. He tried pulling his weapons. Three merchants took him down to the floor before the blades left their scabbards.

As they held him down, Georg moved up, knelt, and cut Fymurip's shirt away from his chest. There, he found only dark hair and skin.

"Where is the cross?" Georg asked.

"I don't have it, you bastard!" Fymurip barked, trying to break free from their hold. "I told you, I serve-"

"We know who you are, Fymurip Azat," Georg said. "We know that you fought against us in Starybogow. We know that you are a companion of Lux von Junker, a man who serves Duke Frederick."

"That is a lie. He does not serve the duke. He serves God."

"If you do not have the cross, then he does. And if so, he is foolish beyond reproach. To take it so close to the duke. Why, the duke may have it already. You may have condemned the world to the fires of hell, Fymurip the Tatar."

"The duke does not have the cross."

"Then who does?" Georg asked.

Fymurip fell silent, clutching the words in his throat. He looked away from Georg and toward Catherine who stood nearby, a blade in her hand thrust forward toward his throat. He glared at her. She matched his gaze eye for eye. "I will say no more."

"Well," Georg said, pulling away, "we will know the truth of it soon enough. Your foolish friend has crossed into France, and there, he will meet with our finest, and he will confess its location, or he and his family will die."

"You would kill an innocent mother and her children for a myth?"

Georg chuckled. "The Cross of Saint Boniface is no myth, as you well know. And yes, I will kill them. To save the world entire, I will.

"Now," he said, grabbing the parchment and tucking it into a pocket. "This meeting is adjourned. Take him, and throw him into a cell, and there, maybe he will remember where he's hidden the cross."

V

He recognized them by their clothing, and by the fact that, as he and his family trotted into Strasbourg, they were on them immediately, encircling their exhausted horses and blocking their path of further ingress. They could have been Duke Frederick's men, but they just didn't have that feel or demeanor about them. Lux could detect nothing supernatural in their stance or their expressions, and over the last several months he had become rather gifted in doing so. These were agents of the Hanseatic League. There was no doubt of that, for what other reason would darkly-dressed men impede an innocent German family on their way into France?

"Hello, gentlemen," Lux said, bringing his horse to a stop by letting one of their assailants grab hold of the throatlatch of his mount. "I'm glad to see that France has finally instituted a greeting party for its humble German visitors."

"Lux von Junker," the man holding his horse said, "you will come with us."

Lux turned in the saddle so that the man could see his sword. He placed a firm hand on the pommel and drew it out of his scabbard a few inches, flashing the steel in the warm sun. "Take caution in your tone, good sir, or that hand of yours will find its final resting place on the ground." Lux climbed off his horse, making sure his son remained secure in the saddle. Then he approached the man, unflinching, his eyes fixed on the bastard's smug expression. "My family and I have had a long, tiring journey, and we require food and rest. That comes first, and then we may have a discussion, if you care to explain yourself, or shall we argue in the middle of the street with blood and blade? I don't think the constable of this fine city will permit such… swordplay in the light of day."

The man flashed an arrogant smile behind a dark, unshaven face. "We have you badly outnumbered, Lux von Junker. You and your family would not survive an assault on your persons."

Lux moved closer until he was standing next to the man. He was a foot taller, and he used his size and angry stare to great effect. Passersby were beginning to take notice of the confrontation. Lux ignored them and smiled lightly. "I can promise you, sir, that not a single hair on my family's heads will be harmed by you and yours, for if it is, I will rip your throat out of your neck and toss it into that fountain yonder, and before your flailing body hits the ground, I will stab your eyes out of the back of your head with my middle finger and feed them to your men, who will be lying in pools of their own blood, shitting themselves and screaming for their mothers. Yes, this is the fate that befalls you and your men, *whoever* you are. So I will say it to you only once: step aside and let us pass."

They stared at each other for a long minute, then the man turned and looked at a companion a few steps away. The companion nodded. The man holding Lux's horse dropped the latch and stepped aside.

The tension of the situation dropped immediately, and the townsfolk continued on their way. Lux sheathed his sword and climbed back into the saddle.

"Do not try to leave town, Lux von Junker," the man said as they rode away. "We will speak to you later."

Two streets down, Rosa sidled up to her husband and asked, "Who were those men, Lux?"

Lux looked behind him. They followed, but at a good distance. "Hanseatic League."

"What do they want?"

"The cross."

Rose shook her head. "But you don't have it."

True, Lux thought, and perhaps their confrontation meant that Fymurip had been successful on his mission. Or, at least, he had not been apprehended or compromised in any way. It definitely meant that the League did not have the cross, did not know where it was, and was still looking for it.

Good.

"We should leave," Rosa said, hugging Adaliz close. "I don't care what that man said. Let us go to another town farther down the road."

Lux reached over and rubbed her head. Her hair was stringy and greasy from travel, but it still felt like silk. "No, my love, we'll stay here for the night as planned. The horses cannot go farther. We'll be all right. I promise."

It was not a promise he could keep, but he couldn't tell her the truth.

*****

A sliver of moonlight cut through the small barred window above Fymurip's head. In the darkness of the cell, he had considered cutting through those bars and getting away. But there was nothing in the cell for him to stand upon to reach the window. The walls were too smooth for him to scale, and they had taken away his blades. For a brief moment, he thought himself back in the pit fights, and he stretched the scar tissue on his back and remembered the scores of men he had killed for the delight of cheering crowds. But this was different. He was in a foreign land, under foreign control. Would they let him starve down here? Would he ever see the sun again, or kneel on a carpet to praise Allah?

He did not need a carpet to do that. It was not ideal to kneel in the dust and dirt of the cell, but what other choice did he have? So, he knelt and prayed, and sought forgiveness for things that he had done in his life, and things that he might do in the future… if he had one.

The latch on the heavy iron-banded door to the cell clicked, and candlelight from outside in the hallway leaked in. Fymurip stood and backed away into shadow. The door opened an inch more, and a face appeared, wrapped in dark cloth. In the faint light, he could not see details, but he recognized her anyway.

Catherine shuffled into the room and closed the door quickly behind her. She removed the dark scarf around her face and leaned back into the door as if she were exhausted. "That was close."

"What are you doing here?" Fymurip asked.

She stood straight and walked toward him, unafraid. *Why should she be? She has all the power.*

"I've come to ask you a question," she said. "Where is the cross?"

"I do not know what you are talking about."

She huffed, and he could not see her smile, but he knew she was. "Don't speak to me as if I am some ignorant merchant. You had the cross before we entered the attic. I know it. Where is it now?"

"I thought you trusted your Hanseatic friends," Fymurip said, trying to change the subject. "Now, they are 'ignorant merchants'?"

"I trust their good intentions. I trust Georg with my life. They *do* seek the cross so that it may never fall into the hands of Duke Frederick and the Eldar Gods.

That is truth. But, they are, simply, merchants, standing alongside tables with charts and maps, with heavy bellies and fat bags of gold. They did not see that… *thing*… come out of the portal. They did not see the green smoke emanating from its depths. I fear that if they were to acquire the cross, despite their good intentions, that it would easily fall into the wrong hands. I doubt that you are the right hands as well, but you understand the foe in front of us, and I think there is a better chance of the cross being destroyed if you are involved. And your Teutonic friend as well."

Fymurip didn't have the heart to tell her that his and Lux's intentions were not to destroy the cross, but to determine its powers, if any such powers still existed within its silver shape. Perhaps after such a determination, it might be possible to destroy it. He doubted it, however, which made Catherine's words sensible. The Hanseatic League might have the best intentions, but did they have the power and influence to keep the cross safe from evil? They certainly had the power in Starybogow, but how far-reaching was that power? Those thoughts brought him to think about Lux. Where were he and his family, Fymurip wondered, and were they being followed by the League as Georg had said.

"How can I trust you?" he asked her. "You barred my escape in the attic."

Catherine moved into the line of moonlight so that Fymurip could see that she was smiling. "Pieces on a board have to be moved one at a time, my friend. If you have never played chess, I recommend that you do so when all this is over… if you survive. In chess, one must weigh one's positional strength moment to moment. I was outnumbered, and Georg is my friend. He's like a father to me. I could not betray his trust."

"But you are comfortable with betraying it now?"

Catherine turned her gaze up to the cold ceiling, as if she were seeking her answer there. "What's the old saying? We who serve a greater good give our masters what they need, not what they want? The trick is making what they need look like what they want. I am young, and I have not had the life experiences that you have had, but I am no fool, Fymurip Azat. So I will ask you again. Where is the cross?"

He stared at her through the darkness for a long time, then he said, "Hidden beneath shingles on the fourth roof of our passing. I could not carry it to your friend and whomever he represented. I was certainly not going to hand it over to the League."

"But you believe me when I say that the League's intentions are pure, and that fundamentally they seek what you seek?"

Fymurip shook his head. "I do not know what to believe. You may be lying to me right now. I may step outside that door and have my neck cut to the bone. You could finish me off right here in the dark; I would never see the stroke coming. I am in no position to judge."

"What makes you so cynical, Fymurip Azat?"

It was Fymurip's turn to smile. "Life experiences."

Catherine nodded, then reached behind her back and pulled out a sword and a dagger from her belt. She held them forward. "Here, these are yours. Come."

Fymurip took his weapons and followed her out and into the hallway. The two men guarding his door lay in chairs as if they were sleeping. They seemed drugged. Fymurip looked at Catherine for an explanation; she gave nothing away in her demeanor. Her focus was moving forward, and he matched her pace.

A left turn, down another dank hallway, then up a long flight of stairs. Fymurip found himself winded as they reached street level and burst outside. Fymurip breathed deeply. The cool air felt good in his lungs, on his skin.

Catherine looked both ways, then led him across a street and through an alley. At the end of the alley was a horse, bridled and saddled. "You can ride a horse, I presume?"

Fymurip nodded. "I am no cavalry soldier, but I can make do."

"Good." She handed him the reins. "Then go, as fast as you can ride, and find your friend."

"Wait! I need to get the cross first."

Catherine opened her blouse. "You mean this?"

There it lay, on her chest, a cold piece of simple, solid silver. Fymurip reached out for it, then stayed his hand. It lay directly on her bare skin, close to her bosom. He had no right.

"Here," she said, lifting it off her chest and removing it from around her neck. She wrapped the cord around it and handed it to him. "It is dead to me. Just a cross like any other. I guess I'm not worthy."

Fymurip took it, unwrapped the cord, and placed it around his neck. "Nor am I. You knew where it was all along?"

"I know my city."

"If you had it, why bother asking me where it lay?"

Catherine shrugged. "I needed to see if you were trustworthy as well. You confessed its location to me. That took courage."

Fymurip nodded. He started to climb onto the horse, then paused. "Come with me. We could certainly use another blade on the road."

Catherine shook her head. "I thank you for the offer, but no. I serve the Hanseatic League. I have a duty to see this through in other ways, other places."

"But if they find out that you have set me free, they might-"

"Don't worry about me, Fymurip Azat. You go and find your friend, and perhaps together, you both can help put this madness to rest."

"Thank you, Catherine," he said, taking the saddle and pulling the horse around by the reins. "I owe you a life."

She smiled at him, then her face lit up. "Oh," she said, reaching into a pocket, "and take this with you."

She held up a piece of parchment. He took it and opened it. It was the half piece from the bishop.

"Take it," she said again. "Perhaps your friend knows what it is. Now, ride! And don't stop till the horse drops dead."

Fymurip nodded and tucked the parchment away. He kicked the horse and fled into the night, out of Lübeck and toward France.

VI

Lux put his children to bed, and then he prayed. On his knees in front of the small window of their tavern room, the light of the moon catching his face. It had been a long while since he had knelt and asked forgiveness. Ironically, the duties of a servant of God could lend itself to all manners of sin, despite what the priests or commanders might say. If a man were honest with himself, he'd have to admit that, at least, and what better way to cleanse the soul but to pray? But Lux did not feel cleansed by this simple act of submission, though he tried. What he really felt was anger. No. What he really felt was rage.

"Don't go," Rosa whispered to him as he finished his prayer, stood, and buckled his sword to his side. The flight from their home had left him nothing else. "Stay with us. Stay with your children."

"I am only going downstairs," he said, "to the tavern, and I will wait there until they come. They will not go away, Rosa, simply because we wish it. They will stay engaged until they get what they want. I would rather face them here than be dogged on the road to Avignon at every turn."

"I cannot survive this without you." She was close to tears now.

"You won't. I promise… just downstairs."

He waited for them at a corner table, feigning to drink a mug of ale in order to keep the tavern-keeper's suspicions at bay. It was a quiet night, thank God, and the few patrons scattered about the room were keeping to themselves and their own conversations. Only one barmaid continually looked in on him and tried to show more leg than he was willing to see. Her hair was dark, but she was pale, very pale, almost sickly, though she fluttered around the room in good spirits, always smiling. She was kind, but annoying. Lux did his best to ignore her.

Three of them arrived. The one who had spoken to him earlier and two others. Lux figured the rest were waiting outside in case the matter spilled into the streets.

"Holding this meeting in a public place," the man said as he approached Lux, "will not keep us from taking you by force if necessary."

"Relax, sir," Lux said, reaching over the table to offer a chair. "You are agitated and anxious. So are your friends. I've seen it a thousand times. Men like you always fall, for they cannot focus their energy into proper action. You outnumber me three to one, and more outside. But I've been sitting here for the bulk of an hour, studying this room, every facet of it, waiting, and I can promise you, there is no scenario under which you will leave this place with your head still attached to your body, if you were to force this engagement by blade. So, please, shut up and sit down, and let us talk to one another like men. And perhaps we can deprive the beast his blood tonight."

The man paused a moment, then took the seat offered. The other two stood nearby, silent, their bearded faces stolid and unmoving.

"My name is Rodrigo Esparza," the man said. "It is my mission to-"

"Spanish," Lux said, interrupting, "and serving the Hanseatic League, no less."

"We have servants from all countries, all creeds and religions. We are more vast and influential than you give us credit for."

Lux huffed. "On the contrary, I've seen firsthand your reach and influence. But I am confused. Why are you harassing a simple man and his family traveling through France?"

"Now it is your turn to shut up, Lux von Junker. We know who you are. We know what you carry. You will give us the Cross of Saint Boniface." The man placed his hand on the hilt of his sword which was buckled at his side. "Or you will die."

Lux paused. He considered reaching for his sword, but instead, he leaned forward over the table, and said, "Why do you-or, rather, the Hanseatic League-want it? It is nothing but a fancy bit of silver."

"It has the divine spark of Jesus," Rodrigo said, "and yet has been corrupted by powers both nefarious and evil. It cannot be allowed to fall into those unholy hands. I think you know this, in your heart. Give it to us, and I can promise you that it will be disposed of properly."

Lux considered Rodrigo's words. He studied the man's face. He had stared many times into the eyes of men less gifted than the one before him, and many times did he see the lies drawn taut and red on those faces. Not this man. He, at least, believed in what he was saying, and maybe he was telling the truth. But with no contact with Fymurip in several weeks, Lux had no way of knowing what the Hanseatic League wanted with the cross.

"I'm sorry, my friends," Lux said, "but I do not have it. It is far, far removed from this place, I can assure you." Lux smiled. "And even if I did have it, I would not give it to you."

Rodrigo stared across the table, his thin mouth twitching. "That... is unfortunate, Lux von Junker. You would not object if we were to inspect your person?"

Lux stood and held out his arms as if he were about to take flight. "You may pat me down at your leisure. You may even stick those tiny hands of yours up my backside if it would satisfy your curiosity. You will find no legendary cross anywhere upon me."

The two other men moved forward at Rodrigo's nod. They patted Lux's arms and legs, his chest, his back. They did not place anything into his backside, but they did pat down the seat of his britches as well. Lux considered ramming his fist down onto the forehead of one of the men as he stooped over for the inspection, but thought better of it. They finished and stepped away.

"Are you satisfied?" Lux asked, putting his arms down.

Rodrigo nodded. "Quite. But there is one final matter we must attend to." He stepped aside and offered Lux the door to the street. "Please, have a look."

Lux stepped to the door slowly, carefully. His eyes instantly found the face of his wife, who was being held by a blade at her neck by one of Rodrigo's men. The helplessness in her eyes, calling out to her husband for help, made Lux's blood boil and his hand tremble with anger.

Lux reached for his sword and Rodrigo grabbed his hand. The Spaniard was stronger than he appeared. "Caution, my brute of a friend. What my man holds at your wife's neck is a *navaja*. Some call it a *santólios*. It is the sharpest steel in Spain, and one nod from me means your sweet wife will have last rites read to her. Your skill as a soldier compelled you to study the tavern; your arrogance as a man left your family unguarded, though your children are safely sleeping still in your room. We are not monsters, Lux von Junker, though you may think it. We are simply desperate men seeking to rid the world of a terrible wrong. So I will ask you now one question, and do not obfuscate: where is the cross?"

"I don't have it," Lux blurted out, trying to keep his voice from showing weakness, desperation. "I-I gave it to my partner."

"Where is he?"

"In Lübeck, or so he was. I don't know where he is now. Perhaps he's still there. You bastards may already have it, so let her go. Let her go, or I'll-"

"What shall you do?" Rodrigo asked, gripping Lux's hand tighter. "Call the constable? The guards? Look around you. There is no one, not even a stray cat, on the streets tonight. We own this town, Lux. No one will come for you."

"I tell you the truth! The cross is in Lübeck. Please, let her go. We can work together, if what you say is true. If the Hanseatic League wishes the cross to be destroyed, then work with me. Putting a knife to my wife's neck will not bring the cross to you. She is innocent in all this. Let her go, and I promise to-"

The wind picked up. It blew down the vacant street, strong enough to almost topple the man who was holding the knife to Rosa's throat. Then several cracks of lightning formed out of the empty sky, near the center of the road, to the right of Rosa, making a concentric circle that hovered there like a ball of flame. The ball grew larger and larger, until it was man-sized. Then a brilliant light leapt out of the center of the ball, and then a dark space formed, like a mirror of fog, roiling like a whirlpool in the center of the flame.

Lux backhanded Rodrigo in the throat and drew his sword. The man holding the knife at Rosa's neck tried to maintain his control, but the black portal in the ball of flame seemed to leap forward, toward them. And then a tentacle reached out and wrapped itself around the man's neck. The man dropped the knife immediately. He tried breaking the grip of the tentacle, but Lux heard the snap of his neck, and then the tentacle recoiled and drew the man through the dark mirror.

More tentacles reached out of the portal, striking at Rodrigo's men, trying to find purchase on their arms and necks, their legs. Another man didn't move fast enough, and he too was drawn through the fog and disappeared in a death shriek that brought a chill to Lux's spine.

Lux moved toward Rosa as she screamed and scrambled away from the tentacles. The wind howled as Lux worked his way through the dust kicked up from the wind. A tentacle reached for him; he drew back his sword and cut it in two. The severed tentacle flopped on the ground like a fish on a beach. Lux drew back for another stab, but the tentacle popped into dust before his eyes and crumbled to the ground in a soft bed of black powder.

"Lux!"

It was Rosa's voice. Lux looked up and there she was, being hoisted into the air by the largest of the tentacles. It waved her around like a doll. Lux held his sword high and raced forward.

Rodrigo slammed into his side. The strike nearly took Lux off his feet, but he recovered quickly and dodged a sword strike from the Spaniard. "Let me save my wife, goddamn you!" Lux shouted over the roar of the wind.

"It's either her or my men," Rodrigo replied.

"Then let it be your men!"

Lux raced to the nearest one and put his shoulder into the man's back. The shock of the strike tossed the man forward, into a waiting tentacle that curled around him like a snake and squeezed until the man's eyes popped out of his skull. It was a ghastly, terrible death, and even Lux would not have wished it upon any foe, even these foolish men. But they seemed intent on trying to destroy whatever horrible beast this was. Lux had never seen such a ravenous creature, but memories of mythical krakens and massive squids came to mind. Whatever it was, no doubt the duke was behind it. No earthly power could summon a dark doorway out of nothing.

He reached Rosa. She dangled high in the air. The tentacle kept her up and out of reach. He tried reaching for her, but each time, the tentacle pulled her away. *It's toying with me*, he thought, *trying to enrage me so that I charge the portal, and then be pulled in with the rest.* But he would not do that. He would not fall for its trick.

Instead, he took his sword and stabbed upward, toward the lighter underbelly of the tentacle. He caught it, but it did not bleed like a normal appendage, and just as soon as the blade punctured its flesh, it healed. He stabbed again and again, and each time the wound closed.

"Lux!"

This time, it was not Rosa shouting his name, but Rodrigo, who had drawn closer to the portal, close to the base of the largest tentacle. "Give me your sword. Mine is not strong enough to sever such a mighty trunk!"

"Get away from there, you fool!" Lux said, now realizing Rodrigo's plan. "You will get pulled in."

"If so, then maybe you will see that I am not the monster you think I am. We are not on opposing sides, Lux von Junker, but my time here is over. My men are dead. The duke has won this engagement. You have won, and you may take the cross to wherever it is you think it needs to be taken to save us all. And I pray that you are correct. Now… *give me the sword.*"

Lux tossed his Grunwald sword to Rodrigo. He caught it just as three smaller tentacles reached out of the portal and wrapped themselves around him. Rodrigo pulled his arms free from their grasp and swung against the larger tentacle holding Rosa. The weight and speed of the blade cut halfway through. A terrible howl echoed from the portal. He swung again, and again, until he finally cut it in two.

Rosa fell, and Lux grabbed her just before she hit the street. The tentacle that had held her fell like a tree nearby, convulsed violently, then faded to black soot.

The three remaining tentacles wrapped themselves around Rodrigo, and with one quick snap, he disappeared into the portal as it closed behind him.

The wind, fire, and lightning dissipated. Silence returned, and it seemed like a normal evening in Strasbourg.

"Are you well?" Lux asked Rosa.

There was a small nick on her neck from the blade, and a dark trickle of blood. She was shaking, and there was fear and confusion in her eyes, but she nodded. "Yes, I'm fine. The children?"

Lux wanted to believe Rodrigo that all was well with them, but he shook his head. "I don't know. Go and see."

Rosa climbed to her feet with Lux's help, then staggered into the tavern. Lux waited until she was inside, then turned and sought his sword. But only the Spanish blade was on the ground. He knelt and picked it up, saw the small spot of blood on the sharp end where it had cut into Rosa's neck. He wiped the blood off on his sleeve, then tucked the knife away in his boot.

A crowd had gathered, having stayed away during the fight, at Rodrigo's warning no doubt. Not because he knew that a portal would open and let out a deadly beast-Lux was certain that was as much a surprise to the Spaniard as it was to him-but because the Hanseatic League had power and authority that reached far beyond Lübeck; though their power could not contain such a terrible beast as the one that had just appeared. Now Rodrigo was dead, or located wherever that doorway led. Were the Hanseatic League's intentions pure, sincere? Lux did not know. If not, then why would Rodrigo sacrifice his life for just a few fanatical merchants? Rodrigo had been foolish making threats and holding a knife to Rosa's neck, but in the end, he had saved her, and Lux too, from certain death. Why?

Lux shook his head. What mattered now was that he and Rosa were alive. His children were alive, and pray to God, Fymurip was alive, and hopefully, already on his way to Avignon.

Lux ignored the stares of the gathered, turned, and walked quietly into the tavern.

VII

Avignon, under the control of the papacy, was a beautiful city that rested on the banks of the Rhône river. Fymurip had never been here before, of course, but it resembled other French cities that he had ridden through on his way from Lübeck. Lux had told him that, in its history, Avignon had once been sacked by Saracens. It had been the center of many battles, many conquests, over the centuries. It seemed peaceful and quiet on this warm, sunny day, and Fymurip allowed himself to relax and move his horse into a pleasant trot toward the city center which was surrounded by ancient ramparts.

Then he felt a deep sting in his left thigh.

Fymurip grit his teeth against the pain, looked down, and saw a long needle sticking through his breeches. The end of the needle was fletched with bright blue feathers. He reached down to pull out the dart, but before he could study it, his eyes rolled into the back of his head, and the earth turned.

The last thing he remembered before slipping off his horse and hitting the street was how beautiful those feathers looked.

*****

When he came to, the big bearded face of a Teutonic Knight stared back at him.

Fymurip wiped his face with a clammy hand, tried to sit up in the cot on which he lay, but quickly fell back down, his head spinning.

"Easy, my impatient friend," said Lux, putting a hand on Fymurip's back to keep him from falling too quickly. "That was a powerful elixir in that dart."

"What is going on?" Fymurip asked. "What is happening?"

"You are in Avignon, and surprisingly, safe. For now at least."

"Why was I attacked?"

"Attacked?" Lux sounded genuinely hurt by such an accusation. "Saved, more accurately. A dark-skinned Tatar strolling down a French street with not a care in the world? That's tantamount to execution, if the wrong ears or eyes got wind of it. But do not concern yourself with any more of that. You are safe. We're all safe, and we have much to discuss."

Lux helped him sit up. An orange was offered. Fymurip ate it greedily, having not had a decent bite of food for days. He drank the red wine given him, letting it drip down his dirty neck. Lux chuckled.

"Easy, my friend. You will eat and drink yourself to death."

"I know my limit, and I am far from it." Fymurip finished off the wine and handed the empty bottle to Lux. "Where is your family?"

"Here," Lux said, "and well, though only by the grace of God. We had… difficult times on the road."

"Tell me."

Lux told him everything, and Fymurip did the same. They talked for almost an hour, detailing as best as possible every aspect of their flights from Germany. At the end, Fymurip reached into his shirt, drew out the cross, and handed it to Lux. The knight took it without hesitation.

"I think it is necessary that I wear it now," he said, "for the rest of our journey."

"You do not fear those doorways?" Fymurip asked. "The duke?"

"Of course I do, but if I am its protector, as Gunter Sankt said, I must begin to act like it. It was necessary for you to hold it to keep it out of Duke Frederick's hands as I traveled back to Saxony, but now we are on another path. Do you trust this Catherine of Aragon?"

Fymurip shrugged. "She is the most capable girl-woman-I've ever met. The question is: do we believe that the Hanseatic League wishes to see the cross destroyed?"

"I don't know. But we do know that the girl put her career with the League, and possibly her life, in jeopardy to free you. Rodrigo sacrificed himself so that we could escape that beast. If this is a clever ruse to confuse us and throw us off our mission, then they are making a big noise of it. We may never learn the truth of their intentions, but I think we can safely say that for now, at least, our true enemy is Duke Frederick and whoever is pulling his strings."

"The Eldar Gods."

That declaration brought a deathly silence to the room. The fact that both he and Lux had experienced the portal and the tentacled beast made Fymurip wish he had never agreed to come to Europe with this knight, and for a brief moment, he wished he were back in the fighting pits. Life was so much simpler back then.

"Come," Lux said, standing up and offering to help Fymurip do the same. "I want you to meet my wife, my children. And then we must go, quickly."

"What about your family? Will they be safe here?"

Lux nodded. "Yes. My friend Barnaul has agreed to keep them well until I return. He has shielded his house with Blud spirits, arcane sigils, and other runic incantations. It is a spiritual fortress."

"And he is a man of God, like you?"

"He was a knight, yes, but he lost his faith long, long ago. Yet there is no one I trust more than he to protect them. Besides, he owes me a life."

Fymurip nodded. "And you are still intent on going to Constantinople?"

"Yes," Lux said. "There, we will find the answers. The question is: how will we get there?"

Fymurip paused as they were leaving the room. "How close are we to the Mediterranean?"

"Not very far. Marseilles is close."

"Good, then let us make haste. I think I know how to get to Constantinople without having to travel by land. That is the benefit of working in the shadows for so many years, my friend. You befriend many, many less-than-wholesome acquaintances. And I'm Muslim. That should give us some credibility with seafaring folk traveling east."

"Very well. We will leave in the morning, after we have-"

"Oh," Fymurip said, interrupting. He reached into a pocket and pulled out the parchment. It was dirty, wet with sweat, but he unfolded it and handed it over to Lux. "I pulled this out of Bishop Arndes's hand. Can you decipher it?"

Lux looked it over, turned it round and round in his hands. He squinted at the writing, shook his head. "I can't make out the script. But the image is simple, if you've been a knight like me and have broken many in your day."

"What is it?" Fymurip asked.

Lux shrugged. "It's the lower curvature of a kite shield."

*****

One, two, three, six broken and burnt bodies-more skeleton than flesh and sinew-fell out of the portal in Duke Frederick's throne room. One body after another, like waste from a sphincter, their burnt bones piled at his feet. The last item to fall through was a Grunwald sword. The girl hiding close by covered her mouth and nose from the stench of it all.

The duke gasped. "That's Lux's sword."

The shadowy man nodded, leaned over and picked it up. His frail body looked miniature behind the long blade, but he held it firm, as if some inner strength was keeping its grip on the hilt. "Yes, but not his bones."

"How can you be sure?"

"These are all men of the Hanseatic League, Your Grace. I made sure of that."

Catherine saw small tentacles reach out from behind Duke Frederick's black beard. She shivered, remembering those tentacles in Bishop Ardnes's chamber. "You had him in your grasp," the duke said, "and you let him go?"

The man dropped the sword onto the ruined corpses. "His death does not serve our purpose at this time. He and his companion are on to Byzantium. To Constantinople, if you will, where they will meet their fate, and we will finally have the cross."

"What are your plans?"

The man shook his head. "The less you know the better, Your Grace."

"You can tell me at least what you have divined from the parchment that you saved from Bishop Ardnes's burnt corpse?"

"Yes. It is a shield, and the Eldar runes scribbled around it told me everything else."

"Speak it!"

The man shook his head. "As I say, the less you know the better. But I assure you, Your Grace, that in the end, you will feel the splendor of what the parchment portends. When the cross and the shield are wed as one, a divine light will spread across the world."

The man seemed almost euphoric as he spoke the words. Larger tentacles leeched out from beneath Duke Frederick's beard, and Catherine reached for her blade. She wanted to strike those tentacles, to cut them away. Or perhaps attack the old, withered man. The priest, for surely he was a priest. An Eldar priest; he had that dark demeanor about him. Perhaps doing so would free the duke from enthrallment. Perhaps it would be best to kill them both. But she stayed her hand. She might be able to strike fast enough to take one of them down, but not both and the four guards standing at attention in strategic locations about the room. She was good, but no fool.

"What is our next move?" Duke Frederick asked.

"Now, you marshal your army," the priest said. "Gather the largest Teutonic force that you have ever commanded, Your Grace, and march toward Starybogow. The last move of the game will be played there."

"But Lux and the cross are headed to Constantinople."

"Do not concern yourself with that. I have seeded the ground there. They will not escape from there intact."

"But if they find out what the cross is-"

"Do as I say… do it quickly!"

The tentacles wrapped around Duke Frederick's head, and his eyes glazed over. He grew still and calm. "Yes, my Lord," he said. "As you command."

They left the room, and so too the guards, leaving the corpses and the sword piled near the throne. Catherine waited a few minutes more until she could hear nothing further. Then she emerged from behind the tapestry hanging on the wall and made her way to the pile.

A cross and a shield. What could a symbol of Christ and a symbol of a soldier have to do with one another? She wondered. And why were the priest and the duke headed to Starybogow? She had imagined that that terrible city had seen the last of this drama, once the cross had been removed from it. She had never been this far east in Germany, and did she dare follow them all the way to East Prussia? Did her service to the League allow her to go there? Of course not, but what other choice did she have? She had already disobeyed Georg's orders by letting Fymurip escape. Would she now abandon the chase, tuck tail, and return to Lübeck and beg forgiveness?

Of course not.

She knelt beside the pile of cuddled-up bones, crossed her chest in prayer for these poor, lost souls, then took the Grunwald sword and escaped through an open window.

PART THREE
The Blood of Constantinople

I

Another three-sailed galiot pulled into the battle as Lux and Fymurip tried fighting off a fresh wave of boarders wielding blood-stained cutlasses and wearing gray tunics bearing the red eight-tipped star of the Knights of Malta. They weren't coy about their affiliation, Lux observed, as he thrust the Spanish navaja into the fresh belly of a new assailant. Whether they were after the cross or not, he could not say, but they were relentless and vicious, as if they had a higher purpose than simply securing pirate booty.

Through Fymurip's shadowy affiliations, they had secretly booked passage in Marseilles upon a ship crewed with Barbary corsairs. They had sailed for a month, and now as they drew near Constantinople, they were being set upon by the *Supremus Ordo Militaris Hospitalis Sancti*… oh it went on and on and on. And what did it really matter? There was no time to observe proper title etiquette. These men were out for blood, and they did not care that he was a member of the Ordo Teutonicus… well, sort of.

Fymurip was fighting off two near a cannon that had been fired once and then overwhelmed by the second wave. Lux had tried for quite some time to make his way through the dead bodies to join his blade with the Tatar's, but the attack kept coming. Already they had lost at least a third of their crew, and even if they won in the end, Lux wondered if they'd make it all the way to shore. He had very little knowledge of sailing. Fymurip seemed to have more, but they were just two men. And now with three extra ships joining the fray, what chance did they have?

The man in front of him sweated profusely, and wicked his sword through the air as if he were batting flies. He wasn't even coming close to reaching Lux, so deranged and fearful he was of the large knight. He was a knight too, Lux supposed, but his frame was smaller, his arms leaner and wiry. The Maltese symbol on his tunic was slashed in three places, and his own blood had soaked through. For a moment, Lux felt sorry for the man, but only for a moment. He waited until the man stepped a few paces closer, then feigned a right-handed strike. When the man leaned in, Lux ducked and drove his blade into the man's belly. The man lingered in death for a few seconds, his eyes widening with each passing breath, then fell dead.

Lux had to give the Spanish some credit: they knew how to sharpen a blade. This *navaja* that he had used since leaving France never seemed to grow dull, but he missed his Grunwald sword, missed the weight of it, the sheer cutting power that it offered in a field of battle. This was not a field of battle per se, but he didn't feel truly comfortable without his sword. But he fared as best as he could, cutting down another, and then another, as the latest wave of Maltese knights stormed over the side of the ship and made their way across the deck.

Fymurip was suddenly alongside Lux. "Where'd you come from?" He asked.

"I saw that you needed help," Fymurip said, positioning himself so that his back was to the small central lateen mast.

"Wrong again, my friend," Lux said. "*Rosa* is hungry, and sharp."

"You've named your blade after your wife?"

Lux drove *Rosa* into the eye of an attacker. He nodded. "She deserves retribution for her trials on the road, don't you think?"

"Watch out!"

A Maltese with a massive club tried roundhousing on Lux. He ducked reflexively as Fymurip screamed the words. The club hit the mast and rocked the sail backward. The lateen pulled free from its rigging and shifted right. Lux dropped to the deck. The man bearing the club was not so quick. The sail arm hit him square in the chest. He dropped the club and tried to hold on as he was hoisted through the air. The free sail hit men on both sides of the fight, then came to a halt as it struck the other sail.

"Thanks for the warning," Lux said. "But I didn't need help."

"Of course," Fymurip said, fending off another attack with a swift slash across a bearded windpipe. "My mistake."

"You seem overly optimistic of our chances. What do you know that I don't?"

"Wait and see…"

Several minutes and three assailants later, Lux heard the roar of cannon.

The three new galiots that had come into battle were not crewed with Maltese knights. Lux did not know who they were, but they opened fire on the Maltese ship. Eight cannons at least, perhaps ten. Each one sounded after the other in quick succession, until the sails and masts and deck of the enemy ship were reduced to cinder.

"See," Fymurip said, "nothing to worry about."

The enemy crew remaining on the deck tried pulling out of the fight, but were cut down to the man and tossed overboard. The Maltese ship itself cracked in two and began sinking.

Lux finished off one final attacker, then fell to the deck, exhausted. He hadn't been in such a scrape for a while. Being aboard a pirate ship could be taxing, but a full-on fight had alluded him for some time. A full fight had alluded both of them, in fact, but Fymurip seemed to weather it better.

He checked to ensure the cross was still safely around his neck. It was. He breathed a sigh of relief, then said, "Who are they?"

Fymurip knelt beside him. "The ships? Corsairs out of Constantinople."

"Friends of yours?"

Fymurip shrugged. "Not enemies, at least."

The remaining crew began tossing dead bodies over the sides. Lux watched sharks gather and begin their feast. He wanted to help toss those bodies, but one of the new galiots drew up beside their ship and locked grapple hooks. When the ships settled alongside each other, three men climbed aboard, spoke briefly with the wounded captain, and then walked over to Lux and Fymurip.

"Sirs," said the one dressed in a bright red turban, tan shirt, pantaloons, gold vest, and red sash. He held a cutlass and a pistol tucked under his sash. "By order of Bayezid II, Sultan of the Ottoman Empire, you are under arrest." He put his hand on the pistol. "Do not try to resist."

It was exactly what Lux wanted to do, and he considered drawing his blade once again, then thought better of it as he surveyed the crews of the three galiots. The men in front of him would fall, that was certain, but the other five score? Not a chance.

He stood, put his hands up in submission, then turned to Fymurip with a wry smile. "Not our enemies, eh?"

*****

They were escorted aboard the lead galiot, not as prisoners exactly-they were not given the indignity of chains or binding cords-but Lux had felt more at home among the dead children beneath the cathedral in Starybogow. These men, nay, pure cutthroats and ruffians, looked upon Lux and his Tatar companion as meat, and for a moment he wondered if there weren't a few cannibals among them. But as they were taken to the prow of the ship and made to kneel there for the journey to Constantinople, he began to feel better. The crew got busy with the work of un-grappling and setting sail. Afterward, they paid him as much attention as they might a stray dog or a wayward urchin. Lux had never felt such comfort in being ignored.

"They do not like you," Fymurip said as he settled onto his knees for the journey.

"They just don't know me," Lux quipped, ignoring stares from the sailors. "Once they get to know me, they'll-"

"They despise and fear what you represent, what that trinket around your neck represents. How many of their friends, their companions, have fallen to Grunwald swords in the hands of knights?"

"And how many Christians have fallen to their cutlasses and pistols?" Lux countered.

Fymurip nodded. "You make a point, but I am afraid you will not have time to assuage them of their animosity. So I recommend that you take care and not fall asleep."

"How far is it to Constantinople?" Lux asked.

"Istanbul," Fymurip replied. "Be careful what you call it around here. It'll take a day, maybe, to get there. By sunrise, we should see it on the horizon."

Lux nodded and felt the hilt of his knife. He was thankful at least that they had not tried to take their weapons away.

The first third of their journey was over calm waters. The galiot rocked no more than was normal for any ship on the Mediterranean, and Lux took this time to study Saint Boniface's cross-carefully and out of sight from any of the Turkish sailors.

Its base was still sharp from its use as a weapon in Starybogow, though Lux could see that its edge was already beginning to show wear. Otherwise, it lay cold and dead in his hand. *Maybe I'm not its protector*, he thought. But it had done its duty in that ruined city. It had helped kill the werewolf and drive that evil curse from the mortal flesh of the man who had carried it. Perhaps it only showed brightness and strength when evil was nearby, or when it was needed to heal and protect. Lux decided to take the artifact's intransigence as a good sign: no one on the ship was causing it to awake. *Thank God!*

He held the cross tightly against his chest and dozed. It was a fitful sleep, and the galiot hit choppy water after a time. Lux was awakened occasionally by shouted orders from the captain. Seawater sloshed over the rail and struck him square in the face. Fymurip laughed at that, and then had to lean over the rail himself and toss the contents of his belly into the waves. It was Lux's turn to laugh, though he kept it low. His stomach was beginning to feel a little uncomfortable as well, but he was managing it handsomely. Perhaps the cross was working after all.

As the sun set, the weather turned once again, and the winds stilled. The captain ordered everyone, including Lux and Fymurip, to the oars. They rowed for several hours until the winds picked up again, and by first light, Fymurip had been right. Through low rolling clouds, the splendid spires of Constantinople could be seen on the horizon.

It was once called Byzantium, and then Constantinople, and now-as Fymurip had correctly stated-Istanbul by its Turkish conquerors. But to Lux, it would always be Constantinople, and he was loathe to call it anything else, no matter how many angry leers or threats he received. It had acquired its proper name under Constantine I, and as far as Lux was concerned, it would never change. It was a doorway from East to West, a trade route and strong military fortress. It had been besieged many, many times in its history, but had only fallen a few. It was a jewel that had slipped through the hands of Christian saints, and as much as Lux respected Fymurip personally, he despised the Turks for their occupation. He did not want to be here, but what choice did he have? Here, he was convinced, lay the answers to his questions.

"Have you ever been here?" Fymurip asked Lux as they were escorted off the galiot and hustled up the pier toward a row of Turkish soldiers.

Lux nodded. "Once, when I was a child. You?"

"No talking!" one of their guards blurted, and popped Fymurip on the back of the head with the hilt of his sword.

Lux rounded on him, but was held back by two other guards. "Hit him again," Lux warned, "and that hilt will be up your backside."

"I am fine, Lux," Fymurip said, clearly wincing from the blow. "Don't get us killed before we take advantage of the sultan's hospitality. He has sent his personal guard to fetch us-all these wonderful servants around us now."

As they drew closer to the waiting soldiers, it became clear that they were not just typical line troopers. These were janissaries, richly dressed in new, bright uniforms, equipped with freshly sharpened swords and daggers. Some even had pistols. These were the finest soldiers in the Ottoman Empire. Luckily, Lux remembered his history. Many janissaries, he recalled, had been recruited from young Christian slaves, and perhaps some of them still harbored faith and duty to Christ and the cross he had borne. As he and Fymurip were pulled up to face these powerful warriors, Lux made a point to show his cross.

They were released. One of the more mature-looking janissaries stepped forward. He honored them with a bow. "By order of Bayezid II, I hereby take command of these men and request that they come in haste to the *Yeni Saray*."

"For what purpose?" Fymurip asked.

The man paused, stepped in front of Fymurip, smiled, then backhanded him across the face. Spit and blood flew out of the Tatar's mouth. Lux, again, tried to respond, but other janissaries were on him quickly.

"To discuss whatever it is that Bayezid the Just wishes to discuss," the janissary said. "Now, if you are finished asking questions, let us go. Take them."

They were seized again and made to follow. Lux looked at Fymurip's broken lip. He couldn't help but chuckle. "Make sure, my friend, that you do not get us killed before we take advantage of the sultan's hospitality."

II

The *Yeni Saray*, or the New Palace, was vast and splendid. Fymurip had never seen such a structure in all his days. He had never been to Istanbul, and those magnificent structures he had seen lying in ruin in Starybogow, or those he had scaled in Lübeck, paled by comparison. He could not help but feel pride in its richness. The Ottoman Empire was doing well these days.

He knew little of Bayezid II, though he had sworn an oath many years past to defend his honor and empire. As their captor had said, the sultan was called 'the Just.' Fymurip did not realize that that meant a swift crack across the mouth from a janissary just for asking a simple question, but he hoped that the incident was behind them. Any further physical assaults, and Fymurip would begin to get mad.

They were ushered through the Gate of Salutation which led to a second courtyard even more rich and majestic than the first. There, they were handed off to a set of nastier-looking guards. They wore very delicate silk of green, gold, and silver, and they smelled of lilac. One might assume that these men had just come from the seraglio, but Fymurip could not imagine that Sultan Bayezid would permit such fraternization with his wives and concubines. Fymurip had to wonder where the harem was. In such a massive structure as this, it could easily be on the other side, far away and out of reach. That was probably for the best.

At last they were taken to a room that Fymurip overheard one of the guards call 'the imperial council chamber'. There, they waited on bent knee.

The last several days had exhausted them both, and Fymurip could see Lux's head bob as he tried staying awake. He was close enough to give him a good stab with his elbow. The big knight almost fell over.

"Dozing in front of the sultan is never a good idea," Fymurip said.

"I wasn't dozing," Lux said. "I was just resting my eyes."

They didn't have time to pursue the matter any further, as a side door opened and in walked a man in the thick white-and-black robes of a grand vizier. Fymurip had never seen a vizier in all his life. He bowed immediately.

"Come, come," the man said. "Both of you… rise."

They did so, and the guards that had brought them there left immediately.

Fymurip thought it bold for the man to shoo the guards away. He held great status and presence, indeed; but under those robes, he could not have been so large, so strong as to keep a Teutonic Knight and a Tatar soldier from escaping if they so desired. Then the man produced a small vial from a pocket inside his robe. He smiled, uncorked it, and let the red liquid inside cascade down onto the fine marble floor.

From the splash of red liquid swirled thick gray fog. Fire and lightning leapt out of the fog as it swirled upward like a tornado. It rose up and up, the fog now glowing brightly as a face, and hands, and legs began to form out of the ethereal smoke.

Then the fog collapsed into itself, and out of it formed a full body of fire, its eyes dark coals, its mouth full of sharp red teeth. Fymurip and Lux both fell backward a pace as the swirling fire efreet rose to eight feet, and then settled into a calm, non-threatening funnel of orange-and-yellow fire.

"I apologize for Ufaj," the grand vizier said, holding his palm out in introduction of his fiery pet. "He has a flare for the dramatic. But he is here for one simple reason: if you try to escape, he will kill you." He moved toward Lux. His expression grew deadly serious. "Although, perhaps not you."

Fymurip could see the grand vizier eyeing Lux's chest, where the cross lay, though it was underneath his shirt. It seemed as if the man wanted to reach out and touch it, but instead, he stepped back and said, "My name is Hadim Ali Pasha, and I am the grand vizier of Sultan Bayezid the Just. I welcome you to the *Yeni Saray*."

"We were led to believe that we would be meeting with the sultan," Fymurip said with as much deference as possible, and with as much respect as possible so as not to raise the ire of Ufaj, whose radiated heat could be felt throughout the room.

"Yes," Ali Pasha said, "and so you shall. But not today. Today, Sultan Bayezid is quite busy with affairs of state, and thus, he has asked me to meet with you, greet you warmly, and provide you shelter and succor. Today, you will rest. Tomorrow, you will meet."

"Why are we being detained at all?" Lux asked, curtly. "We are nothing but simple travelers visiting Constan-"

"Oh, come now, Lux von Junker. Do you take us for fools? Yes, we know who you are." Ali Pasha turned and looked at Fymurip. "And we know your companion, Fymurip Azat. And we know what you carry. Do you think that such an artifact, of such delicate and wondrous powers, would lie dormant on your chest? No. We of the spirituality are capable of sensing such a powerful cross. And now that it has come back into the world, it's important to treat it with the utmost care, and to ensure that it does not fall into the hands of... nefarious men."

"It is a Christian relic," Lux said, "so I hardly understand why you or the sultan would care for it."

Ali Pasha chuckled, showing great mirth, more than Fymurip would have expected. But he was hiding something. That much, Fymurip could read from the man's dark eyes. "Well, I assure you that Sultan Bayezid is a wise man. He will be able to articulate our interest far better than me. His moniker, 'the just,' is no honorary title. You will see tomorrow. Now, come, and let us settle you into your quarters. You may avail yourself to the sultan's hospitality. And you," he said, looking at Fymurip, "may visit any mosque that you desire here at the *Yeni Saray*. I'm sure it's been a long time since you've had proper prayers."

Ali Pasha turned to the fire efreet, who swirled in place just as ominously as when it had been first released. The grand vizier uncorked the vial once more, then spoke a few commands in Arabic. Ufaj immediately began to diminish. It dropped to six feet, then five, then its internal fire cooled and re-formed into gray fog. Then it swirled toward the vial like a snake. It entered the vial, and Ali Pasha put the cork in place. He held the vial up into the sunlight of the room and watched until the trapped fog turned into a red liquid. Then he placed the vial back in his pocket.

"Come," he said again, and they followed.

Fymurip walked slow and deliberate, letting Ali Pasha move several paces ahead of them. Then he leaned into Lux and whispered, "I think we have fallen into a trap."

Lux nodded. "Yes, but whose trap? The sultan's or the grand vizier's?"

III

Their room was large, but modest. Food awaited them, and all manner of plush pillows and silken cloth on which to sit or lay. They ate heartily, letting the juices of the fresh apricots, dates, and melons run down their fuzzy chins. Hazelnuts and figs were available as well. They ate them by the handfuls and washed it all down with wine and fresh spring water. Lux did not realize just how famished he was until the smells of all the fine food struck him as he walked into the room. It didn't dawn on him to even consider that perhaps the food had been drugged.

"I doubt it," Fymurip said, sharing in the dates. "It serves them no purpose to drug us before we have had a meeting with the sultan."

"They could have put something in the fruit to put us to sleep," Lux offered.

Fymurip chuckled. "We don't need anything for that."

And indeed, shortly after their feast, both of them were out cold.

How long they slept, Lux did not know. But a knock at the door woke them both.

Lux reached for his sword. Fymurip put his hand on the hilt of his own blade, then opened the door carefully.

It was four women from the seraglio, or so the petite one, with smooth dimples, pure black hair, and slender body, said. She and the others came into the room without even asking. Fymurip stepped aside and let them in.

They were there to do whatever Fymurip and Lux liked. For the entire evening if necessary. They were from Syria, they said. They had been taken in raids just two years ago, and now they served Sultan Bayezid as concubines in his harem, and it would be a grave insult for Lux and Fymurip to refuse his hospitality.

Regardless, Lux did refuse, though the expression on Fymurip's face made him stop just short of throwing the women out of the room. In the end, he agreed to be bathed by the women, for he certainly needed a bath, and allowing these beauties to perform that duty would bring no insult to the sultan.

One woman helped Lux; three took care of Fymurip. They were nice, submissive, and pleasant, and Lux dozed as the sweet girl scrubbed his back, arms, and legs. He made sure to keep her from moving her scrubbing cloth to places not to be touched. Fymurip did not give such strict orders.

Though Fymurip stopped short of allowing the girls to perform any overt sexual acts upon him, he did allow them to clean him wherever they chose. Lux wondered just how long it had been since the Tatar had lain with a woman. Certainly months; perhaps years. Lux did not know what spoils a successful pit fighter was given, so surely it had been a long, long time for the man. Lux had made a point to be with Rosa the night before he and Fymurip had left France.

The baths were finished. The ladies dried and dressed them both. And then Lux politely sent them on their way with profuse thanks and appreciation to be shared with the sultan personally. The girls seemed disappointed that their evening was cut so short, but they did not press the matter further. They bowed and left.

Once they were gone, Lux and Fymurip ate a little more and discussed their situation.

"We have to leave here," Lux said, "and soon. We have to find the mystic."

Fymurip nodded. "Assuming that he still exists, or existed at all."

"I'm surprised that they have allowed us to keep our weapons."

"We are guests, not prisoners… or so they want us to believe. And so we should act like that until our lives are directly threatened."

"Our lives are threatened," Lux said, spitting a date pit into a silver cup. "Every minute we stay here, we are under threat."

Fymurip nodded again. "Indeed, but this is a fortress, Lux. Guards everywhere, and neither the sultan nor the grand vizier will allow us release until we've met with the sultan."

"If we are ever to meet with the sultan." Lux rose from his chair and walked to the small barred window of their room that overlooked a small courtyard. He breathed the fresh air. He could smell flowers and freshly tilled dirt. "I find it incredulous that a janissary would lie about us meeting with Sultan Bayezid. Clearly we have been intercepted by the grand vizier. And if he is willing to do that, and not fear any reprisals from the sultan himself, then he must be a puppet for the Eldar Gods."

"Maybe, and maybe not. The janissary did not specifically say when we were to meet with Sultan Bayezid. Ali Pasha's intercept may have been the plan all along. They would not want the likes of us to be ushered into a meeting with the sultan without first checking us out."

"They know the cross I bear, Fymurip," Lux said, turning and moving back to the table of food. He popped another date into his mouth. "You heard what Ali Pasha said: he felt its presence. They want the cross. There is no other explanation as to why they have brought us here. I'm surprised they haven't ripped it from my neck already."

"The fact that they haven't done so suggests two things to me. Either they don't really know what you have, and they are being cautious. Or, they are afraid of it, and are again moving cautiously. But we need to divine its full power before they do. And we need to find out its relationship to that sketch of a kite shield… if there is any relationship at all."

Lux nodded. "I agree. But this is your world, my friend. How do we do that?"

Fymurip shook his head and rubbed his eyes. "I don't know yet. I have too much fog in my mind, too much uncertainty. I need to pray."

With that, the Tatar turned to the door and opened it.

"Where are you going?" Lux asked.

"I'm going to take advantage of Ali Pasha's hospitality," Fymurip said. "I'm going to find a mosque."

*****

After Fymurip had left, Lux ate a few more dates, then sat back and began planning his escape.

There were few options, he realized. Fymurip was right: the *Yeni Saray* was a fortress. They might be able to pick their way through the defenses and reach the wall. Then what? Scale the wall? And then where to go? To the mystic's home, of course, though Lux could not remember the man's name, nor did he know his whereabouts. The plan seemed so clear in the ruins of Starybogow. Now, coming all the way to Constantinople just seemed foolish, and unnecessarily dangerous.

He took the cross out from underneath his shirt. He palmed it, held it up high enough so that he could look at it carefully. Still a beautiful thing, even with its sharpened end. But a cold and lifeless chunk of silver. It hadn't glowed since its use in that ruined city. Did it no longer have powers? Had its essence been wiped away in ending the curse of the vucari? Or was it only powerful in the shadows of that cursed city in which it had lain for decades? Lux did not know the answers to these questions, and he wondered if he would ever find them.

But he was here. Fymurip was here. And there was no reason to stop seeking now. If they could just escape, get out from underneath the control of the sultan, or the grand vizier, then they could find that mystic, and they would know one way or another, the power of the cross.

Lux stood and went to the door. It was unlocked. He opened it. Outside, standing on either side, were two guards in full scale armor and sporting heavy cutlasses. They did not acknowledge his presence, and Lux did not speak, nor did he dare step out, though he wanted to. Where had Fymurip gone? Where was the closest mosque in this massive complex? And how long would he be gone? Lux now realized that he should have asked the Tatar more questions.

He pulled back from the door and closed it.

He lay back down on soft pillows. He closed his eyes to give his plans of escape more thought and promptly fell asleep. Several minutes later, the door opened.

Lux was startled awake as three janissaries walked in, in full battlefield attire. They wore a mixture of red and blue pantaloons and great coats. Their *yatagan* swords were sheathed and hanging from belts at their waists. They were tall, muscular, and they towered over Lux in a manner unfamiliar to him. His first instinct was to reach for his sword, which he tried, but the lead janissary held up his hand in peace.

"We are not here to fight you, Christian," the man said in reasonably good German. "We are here to escort you to Sultan Bayezid. He will see you now."

Lux stood slowly, cleared his throat and said, "My companion, Fymurip Azat, is not here. He is praying at a mosque. We should wait for his return."

"No!" The man said, his expression making it clear to Lux that no refusal would be accepted.

Lux considered that refusal, but thought better of it. Besides, the guards outside the door would surely tell Fymurip upon his return that Lux had been taken to the sultan. So, he nodded, collected himself, and said, "Very well. I am in your care."

He followed them out the door. When he stepped outside, he knew immediately that the guards would not bother to tell Fymurip of his whereabouts.

Both were dead.

IV

It had been a long time since Fymurip had prayed in the proper manner to Allah, facing Mecca and going through all the proper rakats-rounds-required. It was nearing sunset, so he could only perform the Maghrib, having missed the first three prayers of the day, the Fajr, the Zuhr, and the Asr. But those Muslims in attendance in the Mosque of the Agas did not seem to care. They welcomed him with open arms, and he knelt with them and shared in their prayers.

He had a lot on his mind as he performed the various rakats in unison with the others. He was out of practice, and some of the words that required recitation took time to remember. But like breathing, the more he heard the words of those nearby, it quickly fell into place:

Alhamdul lil-lahi rab-bil 'alameen
Ar rahma nir-raheem
Maliki yawmid-deen
Iyyaka na'budu wa iyyaka nasta'een
Ihdinas siratal mustaqeem
Siratal Lazeena an'amta 'alayhim
Ghai-ril maghdubi 'alayhim
Walad dal-leen. Ameen

Praise is only for Allah, Lord of the Universe.
The most Kind, the most Merciful.
The master of the Day of Judgment.
You alone we worship and to you alone we pray for help.
Show us the straight way,
The way of those whom you have blessed.
Who have not deserved your anger,
Nor gone astray. Amen.

He said the words once aloud with all the others, and then once to himself, as the prayer came to a close. He felt good, revived, the troubles of the trail washing away with every word uttered. He was at peace. He was among his kind, and it felt good.

Then the realities of his life came crashing back to him. He stopped praying and began to try to figure out how he and Lux were going to escape. For no matter how good it felt kneeling here in this mosque, praying to Allah, he was a prisoner. The sultan or grand vizier could send him any and all the concubines they wished and feed him all the finest foods in the empire. It would not make his and Lux's captivity justifiable, or tolerable.

He left the mosque and began walking back toward their room. He was not escorted by guards, nor was he carefully watched, but Fymurip could feel eyes upon him, could sense that from a distance, his every move was carefully scrutinized. He was not alone, and thus, it would not be prudent to investigate paths of exit. But even as he followed the same footpath through the third courtyard, he looked everywhere, left and right, to see where guards were placed, where the majority of the palace's occupants mingled. And there were indeed 'dead spots,' as a thief he had once met in Starybogow called them: places where nefarious activities could be conducted out of sight of lookers-on. Perhaps tonight he and Lux would make a try for one of those places.

Then he rounded a corner and saw the growing commotion around the door of his room. Additional guards were there. There was much agitated hand waving, raised voices. Fymurip slowed his pace as he saw the grand vizier stooping over a body. One of the guards spotted Fymurip. He pointed a finger, shouted something. Other guards were on him before he could respond.

They grabbed his arms. His right was twisted and put behind his back. Fymurip winced at the strength of the hold. He tried to wiggle free, but the guard's hands were vise strong. They dragged him over to the door of his room. Both of their guards were on the ground outside the room, swimming in pools of their own blood, their throats slit.

They dropped him in front of the grand vizier. The man's eyes were wide, angry. He pointed into the room. Fymurip looked in and saw nothing. Lux was gone.

"Where is he?" Ali Pasha asked, his voice trembling in anger.

Fymurip shook his head. "I do not know. I was praying at the Agas, and you may ask anyone there."

The grand vizier looked as if he were about to strike Fymurip in the face. Then he calmed, looked at one of the guards, and said, "Sound the horn. The Christian has escaped."

*****

Lux knew quickly that he was not being taken to see the sultan. He was instead taken to the janissary barracks, where many others waited. They formed a line on either side of him as his guards led him through the barracks. He almost felt like the sultan himself with so much deference from these men who were, in fact, more highly skilled fighters than he would ever be. But many of them were Christian themselves, or had been at one time, and perhaps they still held some deference to him, regardless of their allegiance with the sultan.

Then he saw a rug being rolled away from a trap door at the end of the barracks. He paused above it and looked down its long, dark neck. Cold air seeped up from those black depths. "Am I to be your prisoner now?" Lux asked them.

"No," said one, handing him an unlit torch. "This is the way out. Follow these stairs down, and then follow the corridor until you reach a small door which will put you outside the wall. It will be dark soon. You will be able to get away easily."

"Why are you doing this?"

The janissaries looked at each other. The leader then said, "Ali Pasha has been compromised by… some dark, malevolent force."

"The Eldar Gods?" Lux asked.

The man gave Lux a strange look, but he then nodded. "Perhaps. If that is what they are called. But it began shortly after it was known that you and your companion would arrive here with the Cross of Saint Boniface. We were supposed to take you directly to the sultan, so that he might protect you himself. But the grand vizier intervened, and he intends on executing you both and taking the cross for himself for whatever nefarious purposes he had devised. We serve the sultan, not Ali Pasha. Sultan Bayezid wishes you to live."

"He cares that much for a Christian artifact?"

The man shook his head. "He cares nothing for it. In fact, had he been able to see you, he might have taken it and ordered its destruction. No. He cares about his empire and the forces that are arraying against him. Ali Pasha appears to be at the head of those forces, and if he has the power now to take the sultan's own guests in his own palace, then it is better that the cross stays in the hands of a man such as you. If Sultan Bayezid cannot have it, then neither will Ali Pasha."

It made sense, but the move was risky. Letting Lux go in the vastness of Constantinople did not guarantee that the cross would not, in time, fall into Ali Pasha's hands, though Lux did prefer to take his chances on the street. But there was a more pressing matter to address.

"What about my companion, Fymurip Azat? He must be released too."

The man nodded. "We will do what we can to keep him safe and to ensure his release as well."

A horn sounded somewhere outside the barracks. Lux had never heard that cadence before, but it didn't sound good.

They lit his torch, and the lead janissary gave Lux a nudge to the steps. "Go. Now! There is no more time for discussion."

Lux took a few steps down, then paused. "I came here to find a mystic. I don't remember his name, but I know that he has great wisdom. He will know what the cross is, and what it can do in full. I must find him. Do you know of whom I speak? He is Anatolian I believe."

The man nodded. "You must mean Azma Sadik. He is well-regarded in the city. You may find his whereabouts in the bazaar that lines the *Mese*."

"Thank you."

Lux continued his descent. When he reached the bottom, the trap door closed above him, and he was alone. He felt a pang of guilt for even considering leaving Fymurip behind. A true companion, a true friend, would not do such a thing. But if what the janissary said were true, he could not allow the cross to fall into the grand vizier's hands. Fymurip was more than capable of protecting himself, and he understood the magnitude of their situation. He had seen what the cross could do in Starybogow. Fymurip understood.

Yet, Lux could not shake the guilt from his mind as he wound round and round through the wet and cold corridor that must have been there since the days of the Byzantines. The subterranean path reminded him of the catacombs below Saint Adalbert's Cathedral. Hopefully, however, this one wouldn't contain any dead children.

The corridor ended at a small door, one even smaller than the trapdoor in the janissary barracks. Lux had to crouch to reach the latch. He pulled up on the latch, and the door creaked open.

Light from the setting sun flowed in, and Lux waited a moment to let his eyes adjust. Then he tossed the torch through the door and crawled out after it.

He was disoriented. He didn't know where he was in relation to the *Mese* that the janissary had mentioned. Didn't '*Mese*' mean 'middle' in Turkish? He tried to remember. If so, then perhaps it meant that the mystic could be found somewhere in the middle of Constantinople. Maybe.

He stood and covered his eyes from the waning light. He was outside the walls of the palace. In the distance, the spires of other prominent buildings were outlined in shadow. It was a beautiful city. He took a moment to enjoy the view, but the sounds of battle behind him, behind the walls from where he had come, quickly brought him back to reality. There was no time for reveling. He had to find that mystic. He had to find him quickly.

Lux kept close to the wall and in shadow. He pulled his Spanish blade in preparation for violence, and he tried to ignore the sounds of cracking muskets and clashing swords that grew stronger behind him. He tried to ignore the nagging guilt for leaving Fymurip behind.

V

"Get your things," Ali Pasha said to Fymurip, "and come with me."

He was surprised that the grand vizier did not seize him immediately for Lux's escape, but he did not argue. He went into his room, grabbed his sword and dagger, clipped them onto his belt, and followed Ali Pasha and his guards across the courtyard to a small antechamber.

"What is happening?" Fymurip asked.

The grand vizier looked both ways as if someone were watching, and then he whispered, "Mutiny."

Fymurip shook his head. "I don't understand."

"Sultan Bayezid has been compromised," Ali Basha said. "The Eldar Gods have influence upon him. That is why I took you and Lux into custody, to keep you from the sultan until such a time as I could figure out our next move."

"But I thought-" Fymurip began to speak. The grand vizier interrupted with a huff.

"You thought it was I who had been compromised, eh? Understandable, I suppose, given the nature of things. But no, it is the sultan. He and his janissary guard have released Lux. For what purpose I do not know. And now they will come for you. We have to get you out."

Fymurip stood there, listening to Ali Pasha's explanation, not sure whether to trust the man. It was difficult to believe that the sultan of the Ottoman Empire could be so easily swayed by supernatural forces. It was far more believable that a vizier would be, since he was much closer to spiritual matters. Who to believe? Fymurip did not know, but regardless of who was conning whom, he could not pass up a chance to leave the palace.

He drew his sword and dagger and whipped them in the air to freshen their edges. "Let's go."

Ali Pasha nodded and pulled the vial that contained the fire efreet, Ufaj, from his robe. He gripped it tightly in his fist, and then led Fymurip and his guards back into the courtyard.

At least a dozen janissaries were there in a semi-circle, wielding their yatagan swords. They were impressive and scary, and Fymurip felt a lump in his throat. Ali Pasha's guards drew their swords. The grand vizier himself held back, having no weapon to defend himself, though the vial in his hand more than made up for his lack of steel, if he so chose to release the beast contained inside.

"Grand Vizier Ali Pasha," one of the janissaries said. "By order of Sultan Bayezid, you are required to release Fymurip Azat into our care. And you will do this now."

"I have nothing but the utmost respect for Sultan Bayezid," Ali Pasha said. His words echoed across the courtyard. "But he is not himself these days. It would be a mistake for me to follow this request, for the end result will lead to all of our ruin. So, I ask you, brave sir. Tell me where Lux von Junker has been released, where he plans to go, and I will forgive you this terrible intrusion upon my person."

The janissary was unimpressed by the grand vizier's statement, and his fellow soldiers moved together, their swords aimed forward, ready to strike.

Though they seemed capable, Fymurip doubted that Ali Pasha's handful of guards could cause much damage to these elite warriors that stood before them. But they made a good show of it, pulling swords and hefting spears. They also had the defensive advantage of chainmail. It would be difficult for the yatagan swords to penetrate the guards' armor at initial contact, but Fymurip knew that that would not last long. The janissaries were far too strong a fighting force to be denied in the end.

A janissary drew a pistol and shot the closest guard, breaking the standoff.

Fymurip charged the closest janissary, as he had done so often against capable opponents in the fighting pits. In fact, he had modelled his fighting techniques after janissary techniques, adding a bit of his own flair.

The janissary warrior came right into the flail of Fymurip's sword and dagger. He moved faster than Fymurip had figured, and connected with the Tatar's shoulder and knocked him back. His own sword was quick and precise, drawing blood across Fymurip's hand. The cut stung like the devil, but Fymurip grit his teeth, stepped aside to dodge another sword strike, rolled and came up behind the man. The khanjar dagger did the rest, finding a soft place at the nape of the janissary's neck and cutting through the bone. The man staggered forward, blood pouring down the back of his shirt, then fell dead.

Another janissary came up to take the place of the one just killed, flashing a pistol. Fymurip was not experienced with fighting men who wielded firearms. Guns were forbidden in pit fighting; no sport of course in being able to kill a man at ten paces or more. The man cocked the hammer, drew it up quickly, and aimed it at Fymurip's face, but a spear from one of the guards pierced his kidney, and the shot went into the ground at Fymurip's feet.

The courtyard was lousy with men fighting, more and more pouring in from side passages, joining both sides of the argument. It seemed as if the entire palace was alive now with battle, and perhaps it was. Fymurip found himself engaged with another, then another, and then a third. He worked his way across the bloody yard, cutting, killing, dodging, weaving, trying to reach Ali Pasha who was encircled by his guard near the center of the engagement. The killing there was high on both sides, the grand vizier's guards fighting like demons to protect their leader, the janissaries no less committed to seeing 'the traitor' fall. For certainly Ali Pasha was a traitor in their eyes and in the eyes of the sultan.

Why haven't you released Ufaj? Fymurip wondered, as he ducked and rolled out of the way of a spear thrust. He knocked the spear aside with his sword and came up and drove his dagger into the throat of the man holding the spear. The man fell dead at his feet. Fymurip pushed him aside and kept moving.

It was foolish not to release the fire efreet. What was Ali Pasha waiting for? And then Fymurip saw why. The fight in the center was going badly for Ali Pasha and his guards, such that he could not even move enough to pull the cork from the vial's mouth. His guards were pressed in tightly; he had no room to pour the efreet out and allow it to grow. In the man's current position, the beast, if released now, would likely wipe out the grand vizier's entire force.

"Pasha!" Fymurip yelled, hoping that he could be heard over the screams and howls of fighting and dying men.

The grand vizier heard. "Here," he shouted, raising his arm up as far as he could, and then throwing the vial to Fymurip. "Take it, open it, and follow. Ufaj will clear your path. And may God keep you safe."

The last thing Fymruip wanted to do was to follow a swirling torrent of fire anywhere, especially one as unstable as an efreet. Jinns were violent, unpredictable creatures. But in the chaos of the battle, did he have a choice?

He uncorked the vial and upended it, letting the red liquid splatter on the courtyard ground.

A gray fog swirled upward, unfettered by the fighting around it. It grew and grew. Fymurip stepped back, and others were beginning to notice this rising mist of gray. Even the janissaries who were engaged nearby made way. One foolishly fired his pistol into the fog, only to have the bullet returned back right though his forehead.

And then Ufaj burst through, his fiery flesh oozing like molten lava. He climbed to eight feet and lashed out with his massive burning paws, scooping up everything in his path, guards and janissaries alike. Fymurip had anticipated such an attack, had seen the creature before, and thus ducked at the appropriate moment. The efreet's arm whisked above Fymrip's head, singeing hair and making his scalp itch.

The battle was over. The janissaries fell back, taking a few shots at the guards and the efreet. Ufaj paid them no mind. His attention was suddenly on Fymurip. He swam through the gray fog surrounding his fire body and placed his smoky-black face in front of Fymurip's.

They stood there momentarily, staring at each other, with Fymurip holding his breath, not wanting to breathe the toxic fumes that emanated from the glowing cracks in Ufaj's face. It did not appear, however, that Ufaj meant him any immediate harm. He seemed curious of this tiny puppet of meat standing before him, wondering perhaps what was so important about it. Then he reared up as if he were a cobra ready to strike. Then it slithered away.

"Follow it!" said Ali Pasha.

Fymurip looked at the grand vizier again. He wanted to say thank you, but saw the wound in the man's belly. From this distance it was hard to know if it was mortal or not. Fymurip did not bother to speak his thanks. He turned and chased after the efreet.

They passed out of the courtyard and into another one, close to where he and Lux had entered the palace. Then the creature turned left suddenly and raced against the wall for about fifty yards. The burning trail that it left behind was almost too hot for Fymurip to walk through. Even through his boots he could feel the sting of scorched ground. But he kept pace as best as he could, thankful that no one else in the palace was brave enough to try to impede their movement.

Ufaj stopped abruptly. Fymurip slid up behind him. The efreet turned and swooped Fymurip up in his giant hand. He fought the beast initially, fearing that he would simply pop into ash by the aggressive heat, but he felt no heat at all. The rock-like smoothness of Ufaj's palm cradled Fymurip like a delicate flower. It felt cool, like a drop of rain. Then the efreet drew his hand back as if he were about to pitch a stone. Fymurip found himself wincing, closing his eyes tightly and waiting for the inevitable.

Ufaj threw him up and over the wall, but he did not let go. The efreet kept holding tightly, and together, they flew through the air, Ufaj's smoldering body elongating and turning into a trail of fire like a flaming barrel thrown from a catapult.

They struck the bay and bore through the salty water like a screw. Fymurip held his breath, held the empty vial tightly, until they came to rest on the bottom of the bay. Ufaj released him, and Fymurip swam up, up until he breached the surface and gasped for air.

The sun was setting. The water was darkening. The wall of the palace was far away now, and Fymurip rubbed water from his eyes and looked around him. The shore wasn't too far away. It would take some swimming to reach it, but once he did, he could go anywhere he wished in Istanbul.

Around him, Ufaj had re-formed into a small puddle of thick red liquid. Fymurip brought the vial up above the water line, uncorked it, and then placed it back into the water in the center of the red film.

Ufaj congealed into droplets like blood. Then one after the other, the droplets swam into the vial like tadpoles, until there was none of them left in the water. Then Fymurip corked the vial again and placed it into his boot.

Fymurip breathed deeply and straddled the water. It was quiet and peaceful here in the middle of the bay. It would have been nice if he had the time to simply lay back and float. But somewhere out there in the city was Lux, and Fymurip knew exactly whom he was seeking. He needed to find the big, lumbering knight before their enemies did.

Who is our enemy? Who is our friend? The questions, with no answers, lingered in Fymurip's mind as he swam to shore.

VI

The Grand Bazaar of Constantinople was the greatest covered market in Turkey, and perhaps the world. It stretched from the mosque of Beyazit and far into the district of Fatih, farther than Lux's capable eyes could see. It swarmed with humanity; and among them were a diverse collection of food, weapons, crafts, silks, wools, animals, and exotic riches from Europe and onward east into Cathay and Nippon. Lux could hardly hear himself think over the sweaty roar of business as he picked his way through a throng of people; hucksters, beggars, prostitutes, old ladies and men barking out the prices of their wares, tugging at his clothing, trying to get him to notice their meager demands. Lux could not help but feel both revulsion and elation; he could not recall anything like this in Europe. In some ways, he felt isolated and alone: he was a hulking speck of white flesh in a sea of olive-skinned Turks; he was an outsider, an enemy. But in other ways, he felt accepted, a part of it, a strand of thread in a long, elaborate tapestry. No one seemed to pay much attention to his skin color for he had snagged a robe from an elderly merchant near Beyazit when the man wasn't looking. He was covered head to feet. Only his hand and his face peeked out from beneath the swallow of brown cloth. The sun had set. It was nighttime. It was not easy to know at a glance who he was, what he represented. No one seemed to care.

Lux did, however, for he knew that the longer he lingered in the market, even in the shadows of night, someone or something unsavory would notice him at last, and he did not have time for distraction.

A one-eyed beggar near the Beyazit mosque had told him of an Anatolian shepherd selling puppies near the center of the market. Perhaps there, the beggar said, one could find information about mystics. Lux accepted the hunched man's suggestion and gave him a copper coin.

Lux now stood a few feet from a stack of cages of yapping pups, a half-eaten baklava in his hand. They were cute. Their faces were dark, their ears drooped.

Their coats were tan to white. Judging from their stockiness at such a young age, Lux figured they'd be large, very large, as adults. Despite himself, he smiled through chewing his sweet meal. The last morsel he held out for the feistiest in the litter to take a bite.

"Don't feed them that," a voice implored from a distance. Lux pulled his hand back instinctively. He even felt a bang of guilt for even trying it.

An old, weathered, thin man stepped out from behind the cages. His gray beard was long, unkempt, and lay on the front of his dark *mintan* shirt like a rat's nest. The *sarik* that covered his head was worn and dirty white. The *dimije* were baggy and rode up on his bony legs. The leather *yemeni* on his feet were shorn and threadbare. He looked positively poor, a shepherd from Asia Minor. Lux was tempted to buy one of the puppies just to give this man some money.

The man put a finger through the cage and let the pups nibble at it. He smiled. "If you do, they'll have the vapors all night. And I shall be the one to suffer for it."

Lux popped the last morsel of baklava in his mouth, chewed, and swallowed. "My apologies. They looked hungry."

"They're dogs, sir," the man said, his voice raspy and dry, but with a hint of goodwill. "They are always hungry. Would you like one? They make excellent guard dogs once fully grown."

Lux nodded. "My children would love one, but no. Some other time perhaps. I seek the counsel of a mystic. An Anatolian mystic, to be sure. I was told that perhaps you might know of one who plies his craft here in the bazaar."

The man raised his brow as if surprised. "Why would I know of one?"

"You are Anatolian, are you not? A shepherd, perhaps?"

The man nodded. "I am indeed, hence the pups. But Anatolia is a large place, sir, and I can assure you, I am not the only man from there in Istanbul."

He nodded politely, then turned and walked away.

"I seek counsel on the Cross of Saint Boniface." Lux blurted the words, then regretted it immediately. He did not know this man, nor was it wise to speak of a Christian artifact in a Turkish bazaar. He knew Fymurip would have given him a stern look if he were there, but he wasn't, and the sun had set, and time was running out. The grand vizier's henchmen were probably out looking for him right now.

The man stopped, paused, then turned. He smiled and offered his hand. "My name is Azma Sadik." He raised his voice so that those nearby could hear. "I'd be happy to discuss with you the affliction upon your herd, good sir. Come, let us discuss it in private."

Lux followed Sadik cautiously, holding his hand against his chest so that the cross did not bounce about too much, as they entered a doorway behind the dog display and walked down a dark set of stairs. The further they walked, the quieter it became, until the sounds of the bazaar were left behind, and all Lux could hear were the echoing droplets of liquid striking iron. The air grew wetter and colder as they descended. Lux paused at the bottom of the steps.

The room Sadik entered was round, carved out of living rock, and was lit by two lanterns that hung across from each other on pegs jammed into the walls. It was a mystic's hovel no doubt, though Lux admitted to himself that he had never seen a mystic's hovel before. But it was no living room or apartment. Nothing lived here except vials of dark liquids strewn across a long wooden table that curved around the room. There was a smell of rot as well, pungent with sulfur, and muddled with the sickly sweet smell of the fur of a wet dog. It would take a while for Lux to grow accustomed to the heaviness of the air, and he hoped that he wouldn't be staying long enough for that.

"You are… the mystic?" he asked, taking a step into the room.

Sadik nodded as he stopped near a three-legged table that sat in the center of the area. On it lay a few pieces of parchment, a dagger, and a bottle of green liquid. "My pup sales are legitimate, and they allow me to eat, live, and thrive here in the capital. But this is what I do best, though such activities must be done in the privacy of shadow, behind closed doors. The grand vizier, you understand, frowns upon such activity. He would have my head for it."

So it was true, perhaps, what the janissary had told him. The sultan was a friend and wanted to keep the cross out of the vizier's hands. Lux took another cautious step forward. "I need answers, sir. Answers about this cross."

He found himself pulling the cross out from beneath his robe. It had been awhile since he had held it tightly in his hand. It felt surprisingly warm and comfortable there.

Sadik's eyes grew large. "The cross… you actually have it?"

Lux nodded. "I've had it for a long time, sir. And I know that, under certain circumstances, it can heal, and it can drive evil away from the flesh of a man. But it has lain cold and unresponsive against my chest for months, and I wonder what has happened to it. Is it dead now, and if so, is it nothing but silver and jewels, something perhaps that I could even sell off here in the bazaar? Or is there some other power lying at its heart that I do not know about? Is it beyond redemption, and if it is, can it be destroyed? I must know these things before I commit my life to its protection. And so I ask you to help me understand what it is, what it can do, and what my responsibility is to it. Can you do that for me, Azma Sadik?"

The mystic stared at the cross as if he were ten years old, and the artifact a piece of candy. He rubbed his face of sweat, cleared the parchment and dagger from the table, and said, "Indeed I can, Lux von Junker. Set it upon the table, and let us get to work."

*****

Fymurip loved the bazaar. He could stay for hours, for days, walking from merchant to merchant, talking, telling tales, haggling over prices that he never intended to pay, laughing, arguing, enjoying life. The hot, heavy air, the smells, the sounds. All of it bolstered his energy, and made him proud to be a part of this diverse culture, if only indirectly. He was a Tatar, of course, and Muslim. He was not Arabic, or Persian. His people had come from the Volga region of Russia, or so his mother had always told him. He had no reason to doubt her; it seemed right in the face of her evidence. He was a Tatar, perhaps more Mongolian than Middle Eastern, but he had served the sultan and the Ottomans as a common foot solider until he had chosen to flee and seek fame and fortune in those frightful streets of Starybogow. And now here he was, picking his way through a sea of people who paid him absolutely no mind, as if he were a neighbor, someone that they knew on sight. He was one of them, and they had no cause to doubt his presence.

That made his job easier, in truth. He could go about his business, and no one questioned what he was doing, why he was here. He blended in like he imagined Lux did not, but he was surprised that he had not yet found the big knight. Surely many had noticed a hulking brute, decidedly European in his demeanor and swagger, lumbering through the throng like some stray golem. But no. No one seemed to notice, despite Fymurip's detailed description of the man. *He's better at the game of stealth than I imagined*, Fymurip thought as he munched on some fried borek. Maybe he had not come to the bazaar at all. The thought of that gave him pause, caused his heart to skip a beat. If not here, then where? Regardless of his height and stature, one man in a city the size of Istanbul would be impossible to find.

Fymurip shook the thought from his mind. No. Lux was here. Had to be. What other place could he find a mystic?

He then stopped looking for an overgrown European and started asking about Anatolian mystics. His search became a lot easier after that.

After a few missteps, a few wrong turns, he now stood in front of a stack of cages filled with sleeping puppies. They were cute in their slumber, quiet, docile. It would be nice to own one, Fymurip thought as he lingered a moment and looked at them. On the kinds of missions that he and Lux had conducted over the past several months, a dog would do well. But he put the thought out of his mind and, instead, spoke to the boy sitting nearby, seemingly on guard duty.

"Young man, I have been told that I can find a mystic here." He whispered the words so that others walking nearby could not hear. "Would you know of such a man?"

The boy looked up, unmoving, his pupils turning red from black. A flash of green scales spread across his skin. He smiled, though there was no generosity in his face. There was only rage, violence, and multiples of sharp teeth.

Fymurip pulled his sword and sighed. *Here we go…*

VII

Lux placed the cross on the table. Azma Sadik eyed it as if it were a piece of bread, and Lux felt a sudden clench of panic. He thought about grabbing it back up, but Sadik did not waste any time. He circled the table, mumbling words that Lux did not understand, and he knew enough of Arabic and Turkish to know that the mystic was not speaking either of those languages. The words were foreign, arcane, and Sadik carried on around the table, poking and prodding the cross to divine its secrets.

He then went to the long table that curved in a half moon around the circular room. He picked up a vial of what looked like an undulating mist. He returned to the cross, opened the vial, said a few indecipherable words, and then upended it over the cross. A green, oozing liquid splashed over the cross and sizzled like meat on a spit.

"That's enough," Lux said as he moved to grab the cross. "We don't need to go any farther."

"Wait!" Sadik snapped back. "We are almost there."

Lux pulled his hand back, and the green liquid continued to sizzle, boil. Lux looked deeply into the smoke that rose up from the cross. Images of snakes and scorpions, of wolves and bats baring teeth, and all other assortment of vile creatures rose out of the smoke and mingled together in a tight-fisted death roll that exhilarated and horrified at the same time. It went on as such for many minutes, and Lux felt drugged looking at it all. He found himself again reaching out to the green-gray mist, as if the mangled faces within were calling to him, inviting him to come.

Then it was gone. The green liquid dried up, the mist fell away, and the faces disappeared. Lux shook his head and regained control of his own thoughts. "What happened?" he asked.

Sadik seemed disappointed, despondent. He shook his head and set the vial aside. "I had hoped for the best, but it is no use. There is nothing good left in this cross, Lux von Junker. Only evil."

"How can you tell?"

"The potion draws the essence of an object out of it. If there had been a spark of goodness within, those evil faces that you saw would have been met with equally determined muses of eagle and hawk, of guard dog, of Jesus himself perhaps. Such a thing did not happen. There is nothing of goodness here. Only bad by my reckoning, and that too wanes by the day. I daresay that by the end of the year, the Cross of Saint Boniface will be nothing more than a hunk of silver."

Lux felt both relief and disappointment. Relief that perhaps he could now pass this artifact over to someone else and go on with his life. Disappointed because he was growing used to the notion that he would be so fortunate as to be its protector for all time. The idea of holding such a responsibility in the eyes of God felt good in a way. But now…

"How can I be sure of what you say?" Lux asked. "Dribbling a few spots of green liquid on a cross is hardly scientific proof."

Sadik chuckled as he shook his head. "My young friend, this isn't science. This is supernatural, mystical, religious. You know that very well."

"Nevertheless. I'm not convinced."

"I see." Sadik rubbed his beard. He furrowed his brow as if in deep contemplation. Then he raised his finger, and said, "Okay, let us try this…"

He went toward the entrance, and there, in the shadows cast by the candlelight, he pulled a cage. In the cage lay a puppy. He brought it back to the center of the room.

He opened the cage and brought the animal out. It lay completely still in his hands. It seemed stiff. Sadik laid it gently down next to the cross. He rubbed it like it was alive, but Lux now could see that it was not.

"This little one," Sadik said, "died just a day ago, bitten by a viper that escaped from a dealer and found its way into my cages. When we found him, he was already too far gone to save. I was powerless to help him. But, if this cross can do what the stories say, then it should bring it back to life. Would you agree?"

Lux considered. He did not know if Jesus or Saint Boniface himself ever intended their cross to be used in such a manner, to bring back the life of a simple animal. But wasn't all life precious in some form or another? It had driven the vucari curse out of that man in Starybogow; surely it could be used to save the precious life of a sweet little dog.

Lux nodded. "Very well."

"Good," Sadik said. "Then you may do the honors, sir. Pick up the cross, and lay it atop the pup."

Lux obeyed, picking up the cross and laying it on the soft belly of the dog. Then they waited.

Nothing, for many minutes. Lux began to sweat, began to believe that perhaps Sadik was correct. Then Lux thought he saw a twitch in the puppy's front foot. Then another. And was that its chest rising with air? It was all happening so quickly that Lux could not be sure if he was imagining things, or if it were actually happening. He moved closer, bent down to get a better look. Sadik did not stop him.

The puppy was now twitching uncontrollably. The cross was glowing. Lux smiled, believing that this test was going to prove him right: the cross was still good, and it could do good things in the face of unspeakable evil. He watched for a little longer as the pup struggled to whimper and regain its feet.

Lux stood straight, about to say something smug about the lack of Sadik's faith, and then a thought came to his mind, one of confusion. He stepped back. "How did you know my name? I never told you."

Sadik's expression changed. Defeat and sorrow were replaced by a smugness that Lux did not like. "I knew your name even before you arrived at my stall. Or rather, those whom I work for knew it."

Lux lunged for the cross and grabbed it before Sadik could move. But it did not matter. The puppy rolled off the table and lay there on the cold floor. It writhed once again, and then fell deathly still.

Lux turned to leave the room, but behind him, the puppy exploded, and from its broken ribs poured a black, sooty mist, and Sadik met that mist with a frightening cackle.

"My master wants that cross, Lux von Junker. And I swear, you will not leave this room unless he has it."

"Who," Lux asked. "Who is it?"

Sadik did not answer. Instead, the black mist from the pup formed itself into a djinn before him, spreading out along the low ceiling like a smoke trying to find escape. But there was no escape. Sadik was right about that. For something in Lux's mind told him to hold, to stand erect where he was, and not move. He tried moving, but he couldn't.

The djinn's face and powerful chest erupted out of the smoke. It bared its long row of teeth and roared.

Lux drew his blade and held it forward, but he had little faith in his ability to stop this beast. He didn't know what it was about to do, but it didn't look good.

I've made a terrible mistake, Fymurip. I wish you were here.

*****

Before Fymurip's eyes, the child turned green, his face elongated, his teeth grew sharp, and his slender shoes ripped apart as his hairy feet gained purchase on the hard floor of the bazaar. It was a basti, for that's the way it behaved. It was not sitting on Fymurip's chest, giving him terrible nightmares, but it smelled the same as the ones he had fought beside in the sultan's army against the Albanians ten years ago. It was impossible to forget a basti, and this one was no ally. It wanted to rip Fymurip's throat out, and it moved to do so.

Fymurip swiped the air with his sword. He knew he wouldn't hit the creature as it bounced from one cage to the other, sending puppies toppling, but striking out as he had forced the basti to cut a wide swath as it moved to strike. That put Fymurip in a better place for a physical attack. The basti did not have a weapon, nor was it inclined to use one. It had teeth, it had claws, and Fymurip had seen what those teeth and claws could do to malleable flesh. It was small, that was a blessing, but it could not be taken for granted.

Knocking over the puppy cages had summoned the attention of everyone around. People scattered as Fymurip moved to counter the beast's attacks. Their battlefield now was a large arena as folk scattered. Fymurip was pleased, for it reminded him of the pit arena near Grodno. There was always debris and dead bodies piled high in that battle space.

The basti leapt, and Fymurip purposefully took the strike in his right shoulder, letting the basti think that it had prevailed. He took the weight of the creature, careful not to let its claws sink into his shoulder, and he rolled with the beast; shifting such that the creature's back smacked hard into the ground. It screamed as its back cracked, but Fymurip knew that that would not end it. bastis were tough, resilient, which was probably why its master had left it to guard the stall. *But where was its master? Where was Lux?*

As they rolled on the ground, knocking barrels and puppy cages everywhere, Fymurip heard a muffled roar from the door behind the stall. The basti heard it too and doubled its efforts to sink its fangs into Fymurip's throat. It was a powerful creature, but it lacked skill and precision. It had grown wild in its attack, snapping its teeth, screaming, dribbling spit onto Fymurip's face. The roar from beyond the door had spooked it, and it was trying to finish the job.

The roar had spooked Fymurip as well, but he had learned in the pits not to move in a rash manner. Thus, he allowed the basti to tire itself out with all of its snapping and clawing. Then he drove his knee into the basti's testicles. Did a basti even have them? Fymurip did not know, but he drove his knee into the beast's crotch anyway, and flipped it up and over.

Fymurip turned, drew his dagger, and followed. The basti tried to regain its footing, but Fymurip was faster, more precise, and he drove the blade into the basti's chest, through the heart, where no amount of supernatural power or essence could save it. The basti wiggled on the blade as it felt the searing pain of the strike leach through its hands and feet. Its eyes rolled back into it head, and its green-hued flesh began to turn pink. The boy was returning, but the boy would be dead as well.

Fymurip pulled his dagger free and let the basti drop. It had returned to its natural state, and for a second, Fymurip regretted killing it. The dead boy now before him was innocent; the basti had merely used his body for its master's nefarious purposes.

Another roar came from behind the closed door, and Fymurip quickly tucked away his regret. He sheathed his weapons, moved to the door, and pressed himself against it.

The roar came again, and then the guttural screams of a voice he knew very well.

He pulled the vial of Ufaj from his pocket. It was clear to him that blades would not be effective against whatever it was that lay beyond this door, whatever it was that had Lux.

Fymurip gripped the vial tightly, stepped back, and then kicked in the door.

VIII

The djinn swirled around him like a tornado. Lux swung his blade again and again, cutting through the beast's horrid face, but doing little damage. The black fog dispersed with each swipe, only to re-form and come on again. The djinn had no substance, and that made it near indestructible. Lux thought he heard laughter coming from that ethereal face, but perhaps it was Sadik's voice, somewhere in the shadows. It was hard to know, and as Lux tried desperately to deliver a death blow to the djinn, he grew weaker and weaker, the creature doing no physical damage, but instead drawing strength from his arms, his legs, his very mind. Lux felt like sleeping. It became harder to hold up the sword.

But he continued to hold the cross. Nothing would force him to drop it. The djinn seemed annoyed at that, as if its purpose was simply to make Lux so weak such that he would collapse and drop the artifact. Lux held it forward like the Spanish blade in his other hand, hoping beyond hope that the cross still possessed some goodness, some trace of divinity that would compel the djinn to disperse to the wind. It did nothing. He stabbed at the beast with the sharpened end of the cross. Nothing.

Lux fell to his knees. It became hard to breathe as the djinn tightened its body around him. Like a constrictor, it choked slowly, until the knight could not move his arms. Lux continued to fight. He snapped his teeth at any wisp of smoke that drifted past his mouth. He spit. He cursed. He did all he could.

Then he closed his eyes. He prayed to God, for strength, for courage, for forgiveness for being so foolish as to come here in the first place, for placing his trust in the hands of janissaries who served a duplicitous sultan. He should have known better.

Lux laid his head back into the smoke as if it were a pillow and waited for the end.

A blast of searing heat struck his face, and the djinn immediately recoiled. Lux fell to the floor, suddenly able to breathe again, though the air was filled with a mixture of smoke and fire. He scrambled backward until he was beneath the curved table against the wall. He rubbed his eyes and tried to focus on the conflagration that swirled in the center of the room.

The djinn was in the throes of a molten beast, its skin a mixture of lava and fire. Ufaj! It had to be. It was the only fire efreet that Lux had ever seen. What else could it be?

Then he saw Fymurip, in the corner of the room opposite his position, trying to keep clear of the battle that raged in the center of the room. The Tatar was trying to engage Sadik, who seemed to be drawing strands of magic from his hands and rolling them into a ball.

Lux crawled out from under the table, rose to his feet, and leapt across the room. The magic balls that Sadik tossed at Fymurip were giving him fits. He needed help.

Ufaj's fire singed Lux's hair as he leapt across the room and into the fray. He used the cross as a weapon, stabbing at Sadik's face. The mystic could not take on two assailants, and he fell back, then fell down. Fymurip took advantage, pressed forward, dodged a final fireball, and drove his dagger into Sadik's stomach. Lux finished him off with a blow to the head.

He stood there and watched the old man die. "Took you long enough," he finally said to Fymurip.

"You left me behind to treat with a horde of janissaries," Fymurip said.

Lux nodded. "I know. I apologize."

Fymurip slapped Lux on the shoulder. "Let us not worry about that now, my friend. We have to get out of here."

"What about Ufaj?"

They turned and looked at the efreet and the djinn, still battling in the center of the room. Their mighty fists pounded each other, and it seemed as if they would be at it for a while, though it appeared to Lux that Ufaj was getting the better of the djinn.

"Leave him," Fymurip said. "He'll cover our retreat."

"How did you come to have him anyway?"

Fymurip gave a wry smile. "It is complicated. Come, let us leave while we can, while-"

Their path up the stairs was suddenly blocked by a black portal, like the one Lux had seen in Strasbourg. Before he could move, before he could even fall back, tentacles reached out of the blackness and wrapped him up.

Fymurip grabbed his hand, held on tight, but the strength of the gory-slick arms pulling him into the portal was too great. Fymurip stabbed the tentacles. Lux did as well, but unlike in Strasbourg, these were thick, tough, and impenetrable.

Lux was pulled through the portal. Fymurip continued to hold on tightly.

"Let go," Lux said as his head fell into the darkness of the portal. His words sounded like a dream, soft and relaxing. "Let go."

"No!" Fymurip's scream sounded distant and detached. "Noooo!"

Lux tried raising his arm to give the cross to Fymurip, but it was too late. He let go, and Lux fell into oblivion.

*****

Fymurip did not know how long he lay there on the cold floor. When he awoke, he was alone, though there were still a few candles lit. His head hurt. His whole body in fact, but he shrugged it off, and rose quickly. Then he remembered where he was, what he had seen, what he had done. He had been pulled into the portal with Lux, part of him anyway, but he could not maintain his hold. He had let go. He had lost Lux. He had lost his friend to some kind of Eldar plane.

He looked around the circular room. Sadik's body still lay there on the floor, partially burnt, all of him covered in a black ash. The mystic looked like he had been dipped in dry oil. To be sure, Fymurip kicked the man twice. Dead indeed.

The djinn was gone. What remained of Ufaj was nothing more than a red stain on the floor. Apparently, they had killed each other in the last throes of battle. What a pity, he thought, to lose such a marvelous champion. But then, how much control could he have maintained over such a powerful efreet?

A chill ran down Fymurip's spine at memories of what he had seen in the portal before he had fallen out. Terrible, dark demons aswirl in the air. Smoke. Fire. Feelings of loss and anger. Hideous creatures or arcane lore. Visages of… what? Ancient gods, lined up like camels in a caravan, as if waiting to walk through the portal themselves. Fymurip remembered seeing all of this.

But he remembered seeing something else that he had seen before. A silhouette of spires in the background, beyond the line of waiting Eldar Gods.

Starybogow.

Fymurip found his weapons on the floor. He picked them up and clipped them to his belt. He did not bother looking at the room again. He took the steps up two at a time, for he had no further need to linger in this bitter, scorched hovel.

He had to return to the City of the Gods.

IX

Lux swirled through the black aether like water through a funnel. He didn't feel whole. He felt liquid himself, his essence spread out like sap oozing down a branch. How long he traveled like this, he did not know. The end of the journey came with him tumbling out the end of another portal and onto hard, dry ground.

His back struck first, then his head. He winced in pain. His head throbbed; not from hitting the ground, but from the images that he had seen. Dark, evil things. Hulking beasts lined up as if an army on review. What were they waiting for? He wondered, though his mind could not begin to fathom the depth of their darkness, their unholy nature. He was glad when he fell out of the stream and hit the ground.

He sat up and looked around. It was dusk, but he was not alone. Before him stood a man in black robes, bald pate, a sinister look upon his face. Beside him stood Duke Frederick, in full plate, Grunwald sword sheathed and attached to his belt, as well as other accouterments of war.

"My lord." Lux tried to stand up, but a sick, dizzying feeling struck his mind. He lay back down.

"Do not tax yourself, Lux von Junker," the man standing next to Duke Frederick said. "You have had a long, difficult journey. Many voices have you heard over these past many months, telling you to go here, do this, run from this, hide here. That journey has come to an end. It is now time for you to awake and rejoin your brothers."

Lux shook his head and clenched his hand to make sure he still held the cross. "Never! You are evil. You have taken my master under your spell." He turned to Duke Frederick and said, "Kill him, my lord. He is a devil, and he is deceiving you. Draw your sword, and end this madness, now!"

Duke Frederick stood straight, resplendent in his war finery. Even at his old age, with his added weight, he still held power and stature. He smiled, and the tentacles beneath his beard leached out unfettered, and Lux could not discern the long, writhing tentacles from the duke's black whiskers.

"Listen to him, Lux," Duke Frederick said, his voice distant and deeper than normal. "I was afraid too at first, my brother, but I have come to accept the truth. A new world is ready to rise from the old… and you will help us see it through."

"Damn you both to hell!" Lux shouted. He turned and tried to stand. Fingernails dug deep into his left calf.

He tried kicking the man off of him, but the Eldar priest held tight. Blood poured from the cuts on Lux's legs. They were painful, but he didn't care. He kept trying to get free.

Then he felt a stillness in his head. A feeling of calm spread through his chest. Like a drug, like opium from Cathay. Lux stopped thrashing. He stilled, and in time, the man released him.

Lux lay there, looking into the darkening sky. The man stepped forward and leaned over Lux. The stranger smiled and held out his hand. "Give me the cross."

It was easy to let it go now. It seemed right, as if this man was its rightful owner. Lux raised his hand and opened his palm. The cross of Saint Boniface lay there, waiting.

The priest took it, then stepped back. "You have made the right choice, Lux von Junker. Now rise, and take your place beside your master."

Lux stood, all his worries, fears, and angers abated. He was again a brother of the Ordo Teutonicus, a soldier in God's army. He stood and walked over to Duke Frederick and took his rightful place at his side.

The duke turned to Lux and said, "I welcome you, Lux von Junker, back into my care. And now, listen as we explain to you what you will do to ensure the return of the Eldar Gods."

Lux listened intently, like a child at story time. And no memory of his wife, his children, or that Tatar soldier whose name he could not remember now clouded his focus. Only the words of the priest and of his commander did he hear, and they were music.

PART FOUR

Shield of Darkness, Cross of Light

I

Catherine of Aragon's stomach growled. She could smell boar burning on the spit in the center of the camp that she watched from secure brush. She did not realize just how hungry she was. The pickings here in East Prussia, under the watchful eyes of the ramparts around Starybogow, were slim. The boar itself turning above the flame was nothing but tough meat and gristle. But anything, even bone marrow, would taste good right now.

She shook those thoughts from her mind. She wasn't here to eat, as much as she wished it. No. She was here to kill.

There were plenty of targets. Rough, undisciplined men of Duke Frederick's Teutonic Army, which had left Saxony under disciplined command. Since they had arrived here, on the outskirts of the City of the Gods, as it was called, something had changed. Now, they seemed lazy, almost lethargic. Or, rather, focused on other, darker things. Things that the Eldar priest and Duke Frederick himself spoke of often around a campfire such as the one before her. Unfortunately, they were not in attendance here. Those that sat around the fire were underlings, but important ones. Ones important enough to die on her blade.

She had followed the army all the way from Saxony, careful to keep back a few miles to prevent stragglers, rear-guard pickets, and flankers from noticing her. She had difficulty regardless, for a woman with the kind of garb that she wore, holding the kinds of weapons that she owned, was an uncommon sight. She had given serious thought to dropping the Grunwald sword that she had plucked from the bone pile in Duke Frederick's throne room. It was heavy and difficult to wield, certainly not for her more slender hands and smaller body. It lay on her back like a thick piece of ironwood. It was a knight's sword, owned by one that she had never met, though had heard about. So why had she carried it all the way here?

Fymurip Azat. The name of that Tatar soldier came back to her time and again in her stray thoughts. She wondered where he was, what he was doing. Was he alive, or had he been killed? She had no answers to these questions, and they informed her judgment more than she was willing to admit to herself. Why should she care about the fate of some foolish Muslim man who had more courage than sense? Her focus needed to be on the men before her, laughing at their own stupid jokes, belching, farting, and making more ruckus than they should in the shadows of those deadly, ruined spires in the distance. They had just come from there, in fact, and had decided to stop for the night. A bad choice, indeed.

There were five total. Three sitting near the fire, peeling strips of meat from the cooking boar. One was checking the booty that they had acquired from Starybogow, which now lay in the back of their wagon, covered in canvas. The fifth was off somewhere in the bushes pissing, defecating perhaps. Catherine sighed. She did not have a bow. She wasn't good enough with throwing daggers… not at this range anyway. She would have to get close.

She took the Grunwald sword off her back and tucked it underneath a pile of leaves. She marked the location with a stick jabbed into the soft ground. She then drew her working sword, the one thirsting for blood. She considered her move and wondered now if they had secured the perimeter of their camp with spirits and other such creatures that might alert them of her approach or kill her themselves. She paused, closed her eyes, and tried to sense anything that might be out there. Nothing came to her. She was no enchantress, nor did she have any inherent connection with the spirit world. But her service to the Hanseatic League had, over time, given her a sensitivity to such things. She felt no supernatural forces here. The ground was barren.

Time to strike.

Catherine inhaled deeply, held her breath a short moment, then exhaled. Then she leapt from her cover.

She made no sound as she rushed the three men near the fire. The blade of her sword was across the back of one of them before the other two realized something was amiss. The man whom she had slashed fell forward, trying to escape, but instead fell into the fire, catching his white tunic aflame, and screaming as the fire leached up his arms and across his chest.

The other two yelped like wounded dogs. One of them turned to her and tried to stand, his stunned mouth stuffed with greasy meat. She delivered the tip of her sword through his throat in response. She rolled with her weapon as he fell, blade stuck in his throat. The weight of her tumble dislodged the blade, and she came up swinging on the other side of the fire.

The third man had time to react. He grabbed a sword that lay in its scabbard nearby and came after her. Catherine dodged one sword swipe, then another, and another. The man was strong, but angry. The shock of her attack had clearly frightened him, and he was whipping his sword around in madness. His broad-sweeping, overzealous moves made it difficult for her to get inside his guard. She tried several times to no avail.

Then his bare foot found a rock, and he stumbled. Catherine leapt in, drawing blood from his neck, and then finishing her strike with a slash to his back and another to the nape of his neck. The strikes did not kill the man outright, but they put him on the ground. He dropped his sword, screamed in pain, and reached in agony for the slice on his neck. Catherine turned from him and headed toward the wagon.

The man there had seen the entire attack, and he was ready. He held a shield in one hand, an axe in the other. He was grinning ear to ear, obviously thinking that she was but a simple girl, and how dare she think she could best Teutonic Knights? He came at her wielding that arrogance.

Catherine leapt at the shield, feet first, trying to shock the man with such a bold move. She was not very heavy, but she hoped that the impetus of the strike would both shock and repel him backward, at least far enough for her to land the first blow. It did not work. He was ready for the move, and he held the shield tightly against his arm and pushed her back.

She fell, rolled, and avoided being struck in the head by the axe by mere inches. The man held a kite shield, and he thrust its pointed end down at her like a hammer. The edge of the shield cut through her arm. She gritted her teeth and rolled again. The man pursued.

She blocked an axe strike. The reverberation of the axe head against her sword made her wounded arm hurt even more, but she bore the pain and managed to reach her feet just in time to receive the man's boot in her chest.

Catherine gasped for air as she tumbled backward and into the brush where she had been hiding. The strike had knocked the wind out of her lungs. She gasped for air. Her eyes were watery from the pain in both her arm and lungs. The fall back, however, gave her time to recover. She found her feet again as the knight sallied forward in pursuit, but his way was hampered by vines and brambles. He cursed and tried using his shield to push his way through the thicket. *What a fool,* Catherine thought as she stood and readied her sword. *You should have stayed in the light of the fire.*

She waited until the man had cleared the brush. She raised her sword up and focused on the soft flesh of his neck, angling the blade such that she'd deliver the killing blow. She shouted and struck out.

A thin shaft zipped past her head and struck the man in the right shoulder.

Her sword only made a small cut on the man's chin as he fell back from the arrow strike.

She ducked instinctively, as if anticipating other shafts from the darkness. None came, thankfully, so she moved in crouch, back toward the light of the fire, until she found the man who had been struck by the arrow.

She ended his crawl with a stab through his kidney.

The reality of the arrow sticking out of the man's shoulder turned her toward the wood. Someone was out there with a bow and with impeccable firing skills. The fifth man? Perhaps, but she had not seem him leave the comfort of the fire with any weapon.

She raised her sword to fight. "Show yourself!"

There was a pause, and then, from the protection of the trees, a figure emerged, wrapped in tan cloth from head to toe. The figure held an empty bow.

Catherine stepped back, her heart racing. "Who are you?"

The figure set the bow down, then slowly unraveled the cloth wrapped around its face.

Her eyes grew wide as a man was revealed.

It was Fymurip.

*****

"What are you doing here?" Fymurip asked Catherine.

"Trying to stop Duke Frederick," she said. "Or, at least, learn of what he's doing."

Fymurip could see that she still had her sword raised, her eyes toward the wood. He shook his head. "Do not fret. The man squatting in the bush is dead."

Catherine breathed a sigh of relief at that. She lowered her sword and sheathed it. Fymurip could see the gash in her arm. "You took out three on your own?"

She nodded.

"Why?"

She moved back into the light of the fire. Fymurip followed. "Duke Frederick has been sending small bands like this into Starybogow for many days. Two, three groups at a time. He seeks a shield."

"I know," Fymurip said.

She turned to him, raised her brow. "How?"

He told her everything that had transpired since Lübeck. She, in turn, did the same.

"I followed the duke and his dog of an Eldar priest here. They have assembled an army-the biggest I've ever seen-for what purpose I'm not quite sure yet. But they seek a shield. That cross that you held once has some significance in this matter as well. The priest spoke of wedding them together. He said a great light would shine across the world once they are paired. I hardly believe he is speaking the truth."

Fymurip shook his head, but did not speak, though the images of those ghastly beasts within the portal, all lined up waiting, came back to him. How much did Catherine, and thus, the League, know of what the Eldar priest and Duke Frederick were planning? Would it be wise for him to confide in her all that he suspected? He decided to keep his mouth shut, for now at least. He had only been in the area for a few days, doing, he suspected, much the same thing that she was doing: hiding, observing, waiting. If she were here, then clearly the Hanseatic League had sent her. She could not have possibly made the trip on her own accord. Could she?

Catherine turned and moved to the wagon. She grabbed the canvas covering the items in the bed and pulled it aside. She revealed piles of booty: golden candelabras, silver cups and plates, rusty-edged weapons, pelts, and bags of gold.

She cursed under her breath and leaned against the wagon. "No shield."

"You killed all these men just to get at their goods?"

Catherine winced as she moved her arm. "Wouldn't you? Killing these men means one less group under the duke's control."

"Killing them will draw attention to the fact that someone, or several someones, is out here killing Teutonic Knights. It will draw attention into directions that you may not like, if he has a whole army with which to wield against his enemies."

Fymurip smiled. "I would have thought that a woman of your thieving skills would have chosen a more-subtle-approach."

"If time were convenient, yes. Time is not convenient, however. Soon, one of these groups will find what the duke seeks. Sooner than we suspect, I imagine. And when that happens…"

She let that last statement trail off as she worked the muscles in her wounded arm. Fymurip nodded. "You need that looked at, cleaned, and dressed."

Catherine shook her head. "I'm okay."

"Come," he said, offering his hand. "My camp is nearby. I can dress it for you."

She was about to take his hand. She pulled back. "Wait! I have something."

She went to the edge of the camp and bent down into the brush. Fymurip waited.

She came out with a sword and handed it to him. He recognized it immediately.

"Where did you get this?" he asked, taking it from her and running his fingers down the smooth steel. There was a fine crack in the blood groove.

She told him. "It's yours now. It's too heavy for me anyway."

"Thank you," he said. "I'm sure he will want it back. That is why I am here as well. Lux was pulled through the portal like those men's bones that you saw in the duke's throne room. But I do not believe he is dead. He had the cross. I pray to Allah that we will find him alive. Have you seen him?"

Her expression changed from one of pain and relief to fear, uncertainty. He waited for her answer.

Finally, she said, "I've never seen Lux before, you understand, so I do not know his face. But… if he is who I suspect he is… you will not be happy."

II

He felt a strangeness that he had never felt before. A foreboding, a fear, as if fear was something that one could feel like a cancer, a knotted ball inside his stomach, right below his sternum. It radiated throughout his body, and he tried to fight against it, but it had a hold of his actions, his thoughts. The moment he took his rightful place beside the Grandmaster, he felt it, and it had not dissipated since.

There was a memory of children, and of a woman fair-haired and beautiful in her nakedness, but he could not find their names among his chaotic thoughts. He knew they meant something important to him, once at least. Now, it was unclear who they were and why he remembered them. He tried forgetting them, but their images would rise up through the whispered dictates of the priest and make his head hurt. And thus he was glad that he was among the ruins of Starybogow, away from the priest and the duke, away from all their demands and those images of tentacled beasts with multiple heads, a thousand eyes, razor teeth, reaching out of the darkness, waiting impatiently, longing to come through the gate. His mission was clear: find the shield to hold the cross. Find it, bring it back to the duke, and all the wonders and treasures of the world would be bestowed upon him. So promised the priest.

He entered the city at the Quay Gate, on a small boat manned by a tiny goblin who served the duke. The incessant chittering of the creature nearly drove Lux to toss it into the water, or hold its head below the surface until the thrashing stopped. Everything about everything seemed to annoy him now. Even the slightest buzz from a fly caused him to rage. All he wanted to do was kill. But he was able to hold his anger in check, stepped off the boat, and only gave the little cretin a backhand that broke a few teeth and sent it reeling backward. He stepped up the quay landing and disappeared into the night fog.

He'd been here once before. He remembered that. And not too long ago. But why? Images of another person, a man this time, dark-haired with olive skin.

What was his name? He couldn't remember it. But he had been here, and now here he was again, searching for a shield. All the other men that the priest had sent into the city had failed, and some had been killed. The priest and the duke were growing impatient. They had the cross; they needed the shield. He had given them the cross after he had fallen out of the dark doorway, had handed it over happily, though a nagging dread of that act bothered his memories, though he did not know why.

The poorer quarters of the city had once existed near the quay gate, along with various open-air markets. Now, it all lay in ruin, in dust and soot, though in his clouded mind there was a majesty to it all, a beauty that one could not appreciate unless he were standing in the midst of it.

Lux moved confidently through the piles of debris, kicking aside dead rats and the occasional bleached bones of thrill-seekers who had met their fate in this very spot. The priest had sent a group into this wretched corner of the city, but all of them had been killed to the man. Funny, though, they had not died here, as one might expect, but outside the walls, in their encampment. Five men dead, and nothing to show for their efforts. The priest was convinced that this was the place where the shield would be found, for somewhere among the piles of detritus lay a statue of Theoderic the Great, in all his splendor, after defeating the Vandals as they tried sweeping through Germany. Legend said that he was astride his black dragon Gorthorax as the Vandals routed south, but Lux did not believe it. The priest believed it though, and thus there was no argument to be made. Lux could not make one even if he wished it, the priest's orders paramount in his mind, and not to be refused.

He stepped up onto a more sturdy pile of broken pillars, careful not to slip into the massive gash in the ground, created by one of the many earthquakes. A piece of the pillar he was standing on broke off and fell into the chasm. Lux grabbed hold of a shard of rock to keep from falling. He waited until things settled, until he heard the rock that had fallen hit the bottom. Then he straightened himself and pressed on.

Up and down, pile after pile of broken buildings and stones, bricks and mortar, discarded furniture which had surprisingly been overlooked by looters and those seeking firewood in the cold Prussian night. At one point, he stumbled into the living space of three Romani who had taken up shelter in the ruins, clearly there to threaten passerbys with ambush tactics. They attacked Lux not realizing the mistake they had made. Two of them fell with deep gashes in their throats before the third realized the mistake, turned, and fled. He left the bodies lying where they fell, and even stepped onto the head of one of them as he continued on.

He reached the steps of an old building, cracked with time and weather, but still passable, though now they did not rise up to a doorway; that had been destroyed decades before by a falling tower. The tower blocked the entrance, and the stairs ended at the chest of a mighty statue. Lux's eyes grew wide as he took the first step, then the second, and then the rest. He paused at the top and stared into the worn, chipped face of Theoderic the Great.

So the priest had been correct. Lux felt a pang of guilt for not believing his master. He should have known that a man of such majesty, such power, would be correct. He made a mental note to grovel at Duke Frederick's feet when he returned to camp, but for now, his duty was clear. He had to find Theoderic's shield.

He pushed himself into the small gaps that lay around the statue. The tower in which the statue had been placed had crumbled to near ash, and the fire damage seemed to have melted the very rock that the great German king had been carved from. Lux's broad shoulders made it difficult to gain entry, but he managed. He cut his hand once when he fished around behind the statue. But he kept seeking, probing.

And then he felt a smooth edge. It was cold like metal, but not sharp. Perhaps the heat of the fires had melted it too, but it was intact. He moved his hand down the edge. He grabbed the item and gave it a tug. Then a pull. Then a yank. He could tell that it was pulling free. He yanked again and again. He smiled. His heart raced. *The shield! The shield! I have it. I-*

"Lux von Junker!"

The voice that spoke his name boomed from behind him. Lux started, dropped the shield, and turned.

Standing there, many paces away, was a man wielding a sword and a dagger. At his side, stood a woman.

*****

"Is that him?"

Fymurip nodded, though he scarcely believed it. When Catherine had told him of a man whom the duke and the Eldar priest had acquired as a thrall, it could not possibly be Lux von Junker, the Teutonic Knight that had been his confidant and friend all these long, difficult months. But it was so. There he stood, as tall and as broad as ever. But there was a wickedness in his stance, a cruelty in his expression that Fymurip had never seen before, and he was afraid. Not for his own life, or Catherine's, but for Lux's.

Fymurip smiled and moved a slow step closer to Lux. The knight did not greet him in kind. Instead, he tensed as if he were passing a stone from his bowel and gave a blood-curdling roar that had no humanity about it. It was as if he were facing the vucari again, and he felt like crying.

Instead, he put up his hands and shouted, "Lux! It is me. Fymurip Azat, your Tatar companion. You must recognize me, my friend. Please, recognize me."

His plea fell flat. Lux's roar petered out, but the man did not pause to recognize anything. In the waning light of the day, Fymurip could see the rage in Lux's bloodshot eyes. Whatever it was that had a hold of his mind, his body, his soul, it would not give in. Lux was gone.

"What should we do?" Catherine asked.

Fymurip moved to the left, mimicking Lux's move to the right. "Draw your sword," he said to her. "This is going to get ugly."

He did not wish to put her life in danger, but he had seen what she could do with a sword, and two against whatever it was that possessed Lux was better odds than one on one. In a fair fight, Fymurip was absolutely positive that he could best the knight. Now? He was not so sure.

Lux pulled his sword, and Fymurip suddenly remembered the one on his back. "I have your Grunwald sword, Lux. Right here. Do you remember it? It was plucked out of your hands by that Eldar beast from the portal in France. You thought it lost forever, but no. Catherine got it for you." He gestured toward the girl. "It is yours again, my friend. All you have to do is just remember. Remember who you were, what you used to stand for, your principles, your faith, and it is yours."

That seemed to pause Lux for a moment. The big man's face curled in confusion, only to be replaced quickly by that same, stern rage that had plagued its lines and curves a moment ago. Lux howled again and a river of spit and phlegm spewed from behind his teeth.

No hope, Fymurip thought, fighting back the sorrow and anger for what the duke and that damnable priest had done to his friend. Well, what could be done about it now?

"I'm sorry, Fymurip," Catherine said as they circled one another on the piles of stone and statue.

"Do not fret it," he said, keeping a careful eye on Lux. "On my mark, we go in together. But let us try not to kill, okay?"

Catherine nodded.

"One… two… three!"

*****

He had always been a powerful man, but now, under the control of whatever it was that the priest had done to him, he was twice as strong. And fast too. Both of his assailants came at him with speed and efficiency, one waiting until Lux committed his attack to the other, and then striking out at that vulnerable moment. For the first few minutes, it looked as if they would prevail, their swords finding flesh on his arms, legs, chest. But the initial shock of their assault quickly faded, and Lux was able to parry and defend against anything they threw at him.

It was clear to him too that they were not prepared to take him down, to apply the killing blow. There was advantage in that which he exploited. He was prepared to kill them both if necessary. What were they to him, anyway? The girl he did not know at all, and so what if the man claimed to have his Grunwald sword? But something about him…

The girl leapt upon his back and brought her sword around to use the hilt to try and choke him. The man moved in quickly, driving his shoulder into Lux's sternum, pushing him backward, but not putting him down. Lux stood like iron, easily tossing the girl over his shoulder, and then turning quickly left to deflect most of the man's wrestling attack. He was good, very good, as if he had had training. The girl seemed to have had no training, but she had natural skills. She reminded him of his own daughter...

Wait! I have no daughter. I have only the Eldar Gods. They are my family now.

The faint, confused memories angered him, and he lashed out, striking the girl in the throat. It was a glancing blow, however, and did not have the desired effect that he wished. She fell back, tumbled down the pile of discarded rock and mortar. She was wounded, choking, but still alive.

That move seemed to enrage the smaller man. "I can kill you, Lux," he said, retrieving his sword which Lux had knocked from his hand. "I can do it easily, you know. I have been holding back, but if you persist, I will no longer delay. End this now. Come back to me. Come back to the world of light, and let us fight together, against this evil, like we did before."

Lux found that the man's words had meaning, a spark of truth, but his head hurt when thinking of them, and the constant babble of the priest's words and the omniscient imperatives of the Eldar Gods swam unfettered in his mind and forced him to rush the man, sword high, and take him down.

They tumbled together down the debris pile, the sharp edges of the broken rock and bits of statue cutting his face. Lux had a lot of lacerations now, though none of them hurt as one might expect. His wounds possessed a numbness that radiated across his body. The smaller man did not have such a salve. He screamed as he took gash upon gash in his arms and legs. By the time they stopped falling, the man lay still, groaning, moving his head back and forth.

Lux, imbued with new energy, hammered his fist into the man's face, again and again, until he held his rage from one simple request that whispered in his mind: *Bring him to me, alive.*

Lux stopped punching the man's face. He stood, pulled the man up by his coat, and hoisted him over his shoulder.

"Go!" the man spit blood as he tried to speak. "Go!"

The girl had recovered and was making her move to try to free her companion, but the man's words paused her. She didn't seem to know what to do, torn between attacking and listening to his command to go. Finally, she mumbled something that Lux could not understand, then turned and fled into the city.

When they were finally alone, Lux climbed the pile again to the fallen statue of Theodoric the Great. With the man slumped over his shoulder, bleeding all over Lux's clothing, it was difficult to focus and find the shield again. But in time, he did. He pulled it out from beneath the debris and held it firm. It was a good shield, strong and balanced. The years had worn its brilliant bronze sheen, and the paint that had covered it was nothing more than specks of red and white pigment along its worn edges. Ancient symbols that he recognized but could not decipher ran its length, carved years ago into its steel. Holding the shield felt good for some reason. His mind was suddenly free of the burdens of conscience, and any guilt that Lux had felt about harming this man, now unconscious and slung over his shoulder, was now gone and replaced with absolute certainty.

He would take this shield and this man back to the duke and to the priest. And then, the world would change.

III

"So this is the great Tatar warrior we've heard about." The speaker huffed. "Doesn't look so great right now."

The voice seemed distant, vague. Fymurip felt the thump of his body as Lux dropped him onto the ground. Fymurip surprised himself by feeling embarrassed, ashamed. He hadn't been in this kind of position, this bad of shape, often in his life; his fighting skills were unparalleled in most cases. He had chosen his opponents wisely. But this time, he had fought against Lux, against a man possessed by some supernatural entity. Lux was not himself, and therefore, unpredictable.

"Who are you?" Fymurip asked. His eyes were beginning to focus.

Though it was dark, they seemed to be in a glade, a bare patch amid a small stone building lit up by torchlight. He could smell horses, and the stale sweet smell of body odor. It was muggy, the air stale. There were several Teutonic soldiers on guard. Beside him stood Lux and a man that Fymurip figured to be the priest he had heard so much about.

"You must be the devil," Fymurip said, finding the strength to sit up.

The priest laughed. Fymurip could hear a spot of tension-and perhaps exhaustion?-in the rough voice. Perhaps he could use that to his advantage.

"The devil is in the eye of the beholder," the priest said, his long, flowing black robe parting as he opened his arms as if presenting something. "I am merely righting a great wrong perpetrated on this world a millennium ago. And you, and your indefatigable Lux von Junker, will help me in that endeavor. We have the cross, and we now have the shield. Soon, when the stars are right, the Eldar Gods will return, and with the duke's army behind them, we will sweep into Persia, we will sweep eastward into Cathay and Nippon, and begin to reclaim the world."

"But you won't stop there, will you?" Fymurip asked. "This Christian army of yours will relish bringing that fight to the unholy lands, and when you are finished, you'll sweep into Europe and crush the very thing that now gives you succor." He turned to Lux. "Can you not see this, my friend? Did you not see those wretched things inside the portal? I saw them, and their intentions are evil. This priest will call them forth, and in the end, they will destroy the very thing you love. They will destroy Christendom, your wife, your children, your-"

Lux put a strong boot into Fymurip's ribs, and the priest laughed. "Take him away," he said, waving a hand through the dank air. "Keep him under guard until we are ready."

Lux grabbed Fymurip's arms and dragged him through the glade, through the cold, damp wild grass and into the stone building. There, he was chained to the wall, thick steel chains like the ones he used to wear for the slave masters. With his last strength, he tugged on the chains, trying to break free. He fell back, breathed deeply, and opened his eyes.

Lux was staring at him through the visor of a helm.

"Do you remember when you broke my chains?" he asked the big man. "Not far from this very spot, I'd imagine. You gave me my freedom, and now look at you. This is not the Lux von Junker I've grown to know and respect. This is not the man I saw put his children to bed in France, nor gently kiss his wife goodbye. Bring that man back to me, Lux. He is still there within you. I can see it. Bring him back."

Lux stood there, silent. It seemed to Fymurip that the man was thinking, teetering on weakened legs, fighting against whatever it was that had a hold of him.

Lux knelt and grabbed the chain with one hand. He then put his other hand on Fymurip's back and drew the Grunwald sword still lying there in its sheath. Then he said, "No, Tatar. I serve the Eldar Gods now."

Still holding the sword, Lux stood and walked out, pulling the door shut behind him.

Fymurip sighed deeply, the pounding in his head growing stronger. He lay back, made a few half-hearted tugs on the chain, and closed his eyes.

How long would it be before the priest made his move? How many days, nights, would he, Fymurip, lay here chained to a wall before the world fell into chaos?

And how did the priest intend on using him to bring those horrid gods back into the world? He had no answers, and no effective plan of escape.

His only hope rest in the hands of a young girl who, he prayed, escaped the dangers of Starybogow.

IV

For three days, Catherine kept a steady watch on the stone building where that brute of a knight had taken Fymurip. Guards were posted in the front of the structure, in the rear, and one on either side. Guards would stream in and out on an hourly basis, delivering food and water, or simply checking to see if their prisoner was all right. It was clear that they had strict instructions not to harm Fymurip in any way, though it did not seem to Catherine that they were doing anything to help dress the wounds that he had suffered in his fight against Lux. That worried Catherine, for although most were minor flesh wounds, such things could fester and bring infection and fever. She had to get in now and save him. But how?

At night, of course. What was the best approach? On one of the sides, naturally. And she had Fymurip's bow, which they had left in camp before searching for and ultimately finding Lux in the ruins. She was not a good bowman; not awful, but it was a skill that she had not perfected yet. Nevertheless, she'd have to use it. That, or face all of the guards at one time… and whatever devilment lay inside that surrounded Fymurip.

She waited till the sun set behind the spires of the city. She waited until the incessant mist off the tall grass began to rise. Such clouds of water vapor made it even harder to find her target, but it would also allow her to miss a few times and not be discovered. Hopefully.

She chose the east side of the house. The guard there seemed the youngest, and most nervous and fidgety. In a way, she felt sorry for him. Just a young boy, a novitiate perhaps, simply standing guard, following orders. But this was war, and in war, she knew, young men die.

She nocked an arrow, raised her bow, and aimed at the boy's head. The arrow flew low, cut through the mist, and fell short. The young guard didn't hear a thing. She nocked another, and this time, raised the angle, and let fly. It arched through the air, above the mist, and struck the ground near the boy's feet. He jumped and looked around, confused, uncertain as to what he had just heard. Catherine nocked another, changed the direction slightly, and let it fly at the same angle. Then she dropped the bow, drew her sword, and ran toward the guard.

Before she reached him, the arrow struck his back. The shock of the strike froze the boy in place, and only a small yelp escaped his mouth. He reached a shaking hand toward the shaft, fell to one knee, but Catherine was on him by then. She grabbed a handful of wet, greasy hair, pulled his head back, and drew the sharp blade of the sword across the boy's neck. She tossed him aside, crouched and waited. She tried to ignore the gurgling sounds of the boy drowning in his own blood, hoping that the sound would not alert the other guards around the house. It didn't appear to be so, but what would she do with the other guards? One was dead. The others, either on the front or back of the house, where the doors lay, needed to be drawn out.

She sheathed her sword and took a moment to consider her options. There were no real good ones, but she pulled a stone from her pocket which she had placed there in anticipation of needing it. She gripped the rock firmly in her right hand. She took a deep breath and held it. She counted to three, then tossed the stone up and over the roof until it struck the other side and rolled down.

There was a commotion at the back of the house. The guards there mumbled something in German. Catherine peered around the corner to see that they were moving to investigate the noise. As soon as they moved, she moved as well, taking the dagger from her belt and holding it tightly. When the guards disappeared, she moved up to the entrance and wiggled the blade into the gap between the door and the frame. She moved fast, punching the blade deep into the wood and working it back and forth to break the lock. On the fourth jab, the lock broke. Catherine moved into the building quickly and shut the door behind her.

The room was dark and smelled of excrement and urine, wood smoke, and stale sweat. She let her eyes adjust to the darkness. A small candle rested on a table nearby, and chained to the wall near the table was Fymurip. He lay in a fetal position. He did not move. She went to him immediately.

She grabbed the candle and held it close to his face. She winced. He was a mess, and in just a few days, his body had shrunk. His skin was wet with grimy sweat, but he was thinner, and weak, a shell of his former self. She shook his shoulder. "Fymurip," she whispered. "Wake up. It's me, Catherine. We've got to get you out."

Fymurip rolled over, opened his eyes. He seemed happy to see her. His thin lips parted, and he said, "Catherine of Aragon? Is it you?"

She nodded. She set the candle down and tried to sit him up. "Yes, now, let's get out of here before they find the dead guard that I left them. Come on, come…"

Fymurip resisted. "No, don't bother. I'm not going anywhere."

She paused. "What are you talking about?"

"I've had a lot of time to think, dying here in chains. I have to let this play out and see what the Eldar priest has in store for me. I have a plan."

"You have a plan?" Catherine rolled her eyes and sighed. "You are chained to a wall. You smell like shit and piss. You are weak, near death. But you have a plan."

Fymurip nodded. "Exactly. I must stay here and get close again to Lux in order to try to break the spell that has been placed upon him. I cannot do that if I go with you. But you can help me. You are Hanseatic League, correct?"

Catherine nodded. "Of course I am."

"Despite our crushing the League's assault on the Citadel, there are still agents in the field, am I correct?"

She nodded. "Probably."

"You find them, and together, go to King Alexander, and tell him my plan."

It was madness. Why had she risked her life coming here if the damned fool was refusing to leave with her? She had a mind to drive the handle of her dagger into his head, knock him cold, and drag him out. But that was madness too. She'd never be able to drag him away in time. The guards would find them and kill them both.

"I can't leave you here," she said, her voice wavering. "I-"

She didn't say the next couple words. She had never uttered such words to any man, and she wasn't sure that she even should. They were from such different walks of life, she and Fymurip. Some might call it blasphemy. It was unheard of, even in the Hanseatic League, the organization that she had given her heart and soul to protect. If she dared say the next two words that her heart wanted her to, there'd be no going back.

"Very well," she said instead, "what's your plan?"

Fymurip told her his plan. She listened intently, careful to remember every detail. When he was finished, she nodded and thought to herself, *Well, the fool has a plan after all.*

Eymundr rolled over, opened his eyes. He seemed happy to see her. His dry lips parted and he said, "Cathrine of Aragon, is it you?"

She nodded. She set the candle down and tried to smile. "Yes, now let's get out of here before they find the [illegible] that I left them. Come on, come on."

Eymundr resisted. "No, don't bother. I'm not going anywhere."

She paused. "What are you talking about?"

"I've had a lot of time to think, dying here in chains. I have to try the play out and see whatever [illegible] has in store for me. I have a plan."

"You have a plan?" Cathrine rolled her eyes and sighed. "You are chained to a wall. You smell like rotten cheese. You are next to death. But you have a plan."

Eymundr nodded. "Really. I must stay here and get close again to Eric in order to try to undo the spell that has been placed upon him. I cannot do that if I go with you. But you can help me. [illegible]"

Cathrine nodded. "I'm one of them."

"[illegible] the Citadel, [illegible] the field and I [illegible]?"

She nodded. "Probably."

"You find them, and you [illegible] my plan."

It was madness. Why had she risked her life coming here if the [illegible] was not going to leave with her. She had planned to [illegible] the head. Knock him cold and drag him out. But that was madness too. Could she be able to drag him away in time? The guards would find them and kill them both.

"I can't leave you here," she said, her voice wavering.

She didn't say the next couple words. He had never [illegible], and she wasn't sure that she even should. [illegible] she and Eymundr could [illegible] even in the Hanseatic League, the order that had given her a heart and [illegible] to protect. [illegible]

"Very well," she said instead. "What's your plan?"

Eymundr told her his plan. She listened intently, careful to remember every detail. When he was finished, she [illegible]

V

Three days later, as the sun set beyond the Pregola River, Fymurip was released from his prison and taken by guarded carriage through the Konig Gate. There were no pickets or Belarus guards this time. The overgrown path from the Pregola to the gate was lined with Teutonic Knights, holding their swords high, making an impromptu archway and chanting some indecipherable prayer that Fymurip-though he was no Christian-knew was unholy. Some foul incantation that the Eldar priest had taught them, no doubt. It was dark, and his vantage point in the carriage was not ideal, but the expression on the faces of these Christian soldiers was clear: they had no idea what evil lay within the words they uttered. They were following orders, as defined by a dark priest and their compromised Grandmaster.

He searched for Lux along the way, hoping that by some miracle his misguided friend would be just one of many in the line. He was not. Only as the carriage wound its way through the ruins, past the demolished town hall and into Igor Square, did he see Lux. The knight was standing guard near Duke Frederick, like a chip of granite unmoving and without emotion.

The carriage stopped alongside a thick piece of marble. It looked to Fymurip that it had been hauled here from some other place in the city. When last he was here, fighting that vucari that had stalked him for years, he did not recall seeing anything so smooth, so large and flat, in the middle of this once grand public square. The makeshift steps that led up the side of the marble to the top confirmed what he suspected: this was an altar, made specifically for this event.

Guards pulled him from the carriage. His hands and feet were still bound in chains. His clothing was soiled and dirty, but that didn't seem to be a problem. Fymurip looked up through the shadows cast by torches that lined the steps leading to the top of the altar. There, he saw the priest, and Duke Frederick, and Lux.

They nudged him with a spear, and under his own power, Fymurip took each step slowly, his feet constricted by the chains. The priest was chanting something similar to what the knights had been saying along the path, but in a heightened shrill that gave away his excitement. The grin that spread across the priest's face gave him the aspect of a wolf licking his chops and watching his dinner graze on the steppe. Fymurip did not look the priest in the eye, would not give him the satisfaction. He kept his head low and took each step as slowly as the guards would allow.

He reached the top of the altar. He stepped in front of the priest and waited. The guards held his arms, in case he tried to attack, Fymurip figured. He had considered it, indeed, but he was weak, without weapons-his sword and dagger left in the care of the stone-building guards-and surrounded by an army loyal to the priest and their leader. He might kill the priest, even with his own hands, but would that accomplish anything?

"We are honored by your presence, Fymurip Azat," the priest said, as if he and Fymurip had been old friends for years. "It is time for you to take your rightful place before your new gods."

Fymurip raised his head and stared into the priest's eyes. They were alert, bright, but bloodshot, infused with a power and glow that Fymurip had never seen in any man's eyes. "I serve Allah."

The priest shook his head. "God, Allah, Jesus, Muhammad. Dazbog, Lacia, Perun, Triglav, and any other god you wish to name. All will be a memory soon… and with your help."

"I won't help you," Fymurip said. "You would be a fool to believe that I would."

"Whether you help willingly or unwillingly is irrelevant."

It was Duke Frederick who uttered those words. Fymurip turned to the Grandmaster and saw the tentacles writhing out from under his beard, like thick, gray fingers reaching out into the darkness. "You will serve us by nourishing their coming."

Lux moved forward, his old Grunwald sword firmly grasped in his large hands. Fymurip was glad to see that, at least.

The priest chuckled. "You see, everyone wishes your help. Even an old friend."

"What do you intend for me to do?" Fymurip asked. "Give you good tidings? Provide moral support? Hand you the cross?"

The priest moved forward until his face was mere inches away. Fymurip considered spitting in his eye, but why waste good spit on the likes of this foul creature? He deserved nothing.

"All I need is your flesh," the priest said. He nodded to the guards, and they seized Fymurip.

He struggled, but their grip was too strong, and they dragged him to the edge of the altar where a stone archway had been erected. He was placed inside the archway where more chains waited. He was hoisted up, and the guards wrapped the archway chains around his arms and legs. They pulled him taut, like a pelt being stretched to dry. Fymurip struggled against the chains, suddenly regretting his decision to allow Catherine to leave the stone building without him. *I'm a fool,* he thought as he looked down onto Igor Square.

Below him, in a place cleared of debris, was another archway. This one was twice as large as the one Fymurip was chained in, and it lay angled backward so that the object in its center was facing the sky. That object was the shield that Lux had pulled from the ruins days ago.

Four holes had been punctured into its thick steel, and chains had been run through them. The shield lay stretched in the center like Fymurip, but it glowed a ghastly green and blue that cast light into the shadows nearby.

Catherine, where are you?

The priest walked carefully down the make-shift steps and crossed the small space between the altar and where the shield lay. He had the cross of Saint Boniface in his hand, and he waved it back and forth before him like incense. It too shone brightly, a strong white light emanating from its smooth silver. Fymurip's eyes grew large. It was the first time the cross had shone life since its use in the Citadel against the vucari. Fymurip could not decide if that was good or bad. The fact that it was glowing did not seem to affect the priest in any way. He held it firmly, and it did not seem to burn him or make him retch, and Fymurip's heart sank as he watched the priest cover the space, walk up to the shield, and stand before it.

He held the cross high. "You have waited long enough for your return, my masters. And with this cross… with this shield… you will reclaim the world for your own. The stars are right! Now come… come back to us, and lead my army to victory."

"Did you hear him, Duke Frederick?" Fymurip shouted over the growing wind. Dark clouds gathered in the sky above; a shot of lightning spread through them.

"He does not consider you or Lux equals in this endeavor. You are his servants, his slaves. *His* gods will come, and they will sweep across this city, and they will kill everything. They will kill *your* army, and your power will abate from the world. Seize him… and end this now!"

His words were lost in the wind that blew against his face sharp and painful. Specks of sand, dirt, chips of discarded stone, and all other manner of waste flew into his face and past him as the clouds grew darker, the winds more intense, the lightning more intense. Below him, the priest laughed.

"Spare us your pieties, Tatar," the priest said. "It is too late for such theatrics. Now is the time of reckoning. Now, they come!"

The priest turned from Fymurip, brought the cross to his lips. He kissed it, held it against his head, and then placed it in the center of the shield.

For a moment, nothing happened. Then, the light in the cross grew darker, subdued, with green and blue tints. Fymurip struggled against his chains, cried out to Lux and the duke, pleading with them to end this madness. But they stood there behind him, stolid and unspeaking, watching the green-blue light swirl up like smoke from where the cross touched the shield.

Fymurip watched as the priest, now shouting his horrid incantations, fell back from the growing light. Lightning struck the ground near the priest's feet, but he was not electrocuted. Instead, a bolt of light spread through the ground and around the archway where the shield and cross lay.

Lightning struck the shield, and it exploded into a massive ray of green, blue, and white light. The light shot into the sky. Fymurip turned his head from the flash and the heat. The wind now was unbearable. Fymurip fought to open his eyes to see what was happening, but all he could see was light. It was as if the sun itself had set down in the middle of Igor Square.

Then as fast as it appeared, it was gone. A long minute passed in silence. Fymurip dared to open his eyes. He opened his mouth to speak again, and then the shield erupted once more. But this time, there was no light. There was only darkness, a thick, deep, choking darkness that rolled out of the cross and shield like a fog. The darkness swirled into a circle and became a portal, like the one he had seen in the mystic's hovel. But this one was ten times larger, and the eyes that peered out of it were terrifying.

Fymurip laid his head back and screamed.

*****

The scream was recognizable to Lux. He had heard that voice before, though never in such distress. He did not know why, but the sound of it, lifting above the roar of the wind and lightning strikes, scared him. It made him fall back even further from his honored position at the right hand of Duke Frederick. The man chained to the archway screamed again as tentacles reached out of the dark portal and wrapped themselves around him.

Lux had never felt such mixed emotions. The screaming of the man; the coming of the Eldar Gods; the honor of serving the duke. All of these things demanded his attention, and he did not know what to do. The imperative in his mind held him firm in his place, but his heart called out to the man screaming. The man screamed "Lux! Lux! Lux!" over and over as the tentacles of the first glorious Eldar God pulled the man free from his chains and drew him close to the darkness of the doorway between this world and theirs.

"Now, feast!" The Eldar priest said, throwing his arms up toward the heavens as if he were in prayer. "Take this sinful man's flesh and feast upon it. Gain your strength, O Glorious One, and return to the earth!"

The pustule, bulbous head of the first god peeked out of the dark portal. There was no form to it. The flesh of its face melted and re-formed, melted and re-formed again in various shapes and sizes, but always lined with multiple rows of razor teeth, both black and bleach bone white, snapping in powerful jaws that frightened even Lux. How wonderful it was. How glorious, as the priest had said. And yet…

Lux moved forward and instinctively his hand went to his Grunwald sword. *That's right*, he thought, as he felt the smooth pommel of his weapon. The screaming man had given it to him. But how had he gotten it in the first place? How…

He drew his sword and stepped in front of the duke. "Step aside," the duke said, placing his hand on Lux's back. "I cannot see."

Lux turned and opened his mouth to speak defiance to the Grandmaster's order, but a shaft came out of the darkness and struck the duke in the shoulder. Then another and another. A shaft struck Lux, and he dropped to the altar.

The air now was alive with arrows, coming from everywhere. And then screaming and howling, but not from the man in the Eldar God's clutch. These were singular, high-pitched screams, like a howling horde on a charge.

Then he saw them. Scores of wolves with tiny green riders atop black leather saddles, pouring out of the shadows, out of the gaps between ruined walls and buildings. Goblin conscripts risen through ancient incantations of the Old Gods and servants of King Alexander. But that was not all. Behind them, in loose ranks three deep, came Muscovite spearmen, Poles and Romani swordsmen. More men than the few scant Teutonic Knights that the Grandmaster brought with him into Starybogow. Lux could see immediately that his side was outnumbered.

My side?

As the goblins leapt off their wolves and upon the gray tentacles of the Eldar God trying to emerge from the portal, Lux was no longer certain which side he belonged to. His mind and his body hurt, and he flailed on the ground, trying to strike back at the wolves and goblins that swarmed his position trying desperately to get at the duke who lay beside him, wounded and bleeding. He knew that he must protect the Grandmaster, but that loyalty did not come from the commands of the Eldar priest, who Lux could now see was trying to protect himself from Romani killers. No. It came from the simple truth that he was, in the end, a Christian soldier. A Teutonic Knight.

All his memories from the past year flooded back to him. All the adventures. The pain. The suffering. The victories. The defeats. Images of his wife. His children. He once again knew who he was, and why he was here. Not to be a slave to an Eldar priest. Suddenly, his purpose was clear, and it lay in the face of the screaming man still wrapped in gray tentacles.

There was a woman dangling on a spear that had been thrust into the Eldar God's mouth. Somehow, Lux recognized her as well, though her face was not as clear to him as the screaming man's. The man's name eluded him still, but they were friends. He knew that much. And his friend needed help.

Finding renewed strength, Lux pushed away the mass of goblins and wolves that were heaped upon the altar. They scattered before him as he swept his sword left then right, cutting a swath through their gory bodies with ease. He took to the stairs downward and the enemy horde shifted its focus on the other knights that were still fighting to protect the duke. The knights were outnumbered, but they were of the Ordo Teutonicus, and they fought hard and bravely. Lux ignored them and made his way to the portal.

The woman had fallen off the spear as it cracked in half. She seemed to be unconscious as she lay there before the portal. The Eldar God, which had shifted most of its body out of the portal was struggling with dozens of goblins clawing and biting at its tentacles, but it was faring well. Too well in Lux's opinion, as more of his recollection of events came flooding back to him through faint memories.

He reached the Eldar God, and swung his sword at a thick, writhing tentacle that squeezed three goblins in its grasp. There was no saving them; their red, bulbous eyes were flopping out of their sockets as the tentacle continued to constrict around their frail bodies. But Lux's sword swipe cut a deep gash in the gray, gooey flesh of the creature.

The thick, sharp beak of the god snapped heads off each goblin in turn. It was as if the wound from Lux's sword attack had done nothing to stay the thing from continuing its killing path out of the portal. Lux hacked again and again, spreading out his attack, working his way around each tentacle to try and reach the screaming man before his eyes were bulging out of his head like those poor little goblins.

Unlike the goblins, whose strength lay in their numbers, the man was a trained killer. Lux could see that immediately. The man held no weapons, but he refused to remain still and let the tentacle draw him toward the bloody, snapping beak. Lux continued his move, slashing as he went, finding soft spots along the tentacles to do the most damage. He was doing a sizable amount of damage, too, but the creature was large, larger than those scant tentacles he remembered now seeing coming out of the smaller portal in France.

He reached the screaming man, and over the chaos, he heard the man's voice and saw his wild motions with bloody hands. Lux ducked a sweeping tentacle and heard the desperate words, "Give me your sword!" *My sword?* He looked up and saw the man gesturing frantically with his hands to toss up the blade. *Is he insane?* Lux was not about to give up his only weapon. But wait: he did have a blade at his side. Lux remembered the knife now, a Spanish blade, unhooked it from his belt, and tossed it up. The man caught it easily and quickly began jamming the steel hilt deep into the tentacle that squeezed him.

A fist landed square on the left side of Lux's face. The speed and shock of the blow sent him backward, though he maintained his footing, turned and held up his sword in defense.

It was the Eldar priest, the front of his robe and his face covered in Moscovite blood. He was screaming inaudible things into Lux's face, his wild eyes rolling backward into his head. Lux took another step back and felt a tendril of suggestion leaching through his mind. He knew immediately what it was: the priest was trying to regain his control over Lux. How he could even consider such a move in the midst of so much chaos, Lux could not divine. But he was trying.

Lux raised his sword and tried to bring it down on top of the priest's head. A tentacle struck out and knocked the blow aside. Lux tried again and failed. The power of the priest's control began to tug at Lux's thoughts, but this time, Lux was stronger and refused to obey. Though he could not strike down the priest, the madness that was occurring all around was just enough distraction that the priest could not get full control of Lux again, and he took this opportunity to do what had to be done.

Lux rushed the portal. The light and heat emanating from it were near unbearable, but there was no other way of ending this. In truth, Lux was not sure even if this move would bring an end to the seeming standstill, but he had to try.

He cut his way through the thick tentacles, accepting splash after splash of gory green and gray blood that pulsed from each gaping wound he delivered to the creature. The creature roared in its pain, but kept trying to pull its way fully out of the portal. Lux could now see the fish-like head of the next god in line, peeking out from behind the hindquarters of the god in front of it, and he knew there were others waiting as well. There was no other way to end this but to rush the portal and…

He saw the cross now, a dark outline glowing at the top of the shield. Its silver facade seemed almost dark against the bursting light from the portal, and Lux thanked God for it. He could see the cross in full.

He put a boot against a tentacle and propelled himself upward as if he were stepping up a ladder. The thick arms of the creature made perfect steps up to the shield. The way was slimy, and Lux misstepped once, but managed to keep his balance by sliding his sword into the thick flesh of a tentacle. He pulled himself up and into the searing light of the portal.

He could almost feel his flesh peeling from his face. It was impossible to keep his eyes open, and so he closed them and reached up through the light and heat, extending his fingers toward the cross. He ignored the smell of his singed skin and beard and kept reaching.

And there it was. The cross was now in his hand, and it was not hot, but cool. He recognized the shape of it immediately, remembering how it had felt in his hand before, remembering how he had used it to kill the vucari in this very city. That memory seemed so long ago, but he clung to it, much like how he was clinging to the cross now.

He pulled on it. It did not give. He pulled again, and again, and again, until it felt as if his arm would rip from its socket. He screamed. He shouted. He howled. Then he prayed, harder than he had ever done so in his life, opening his mind to the divine power of Christ, until finally, through his strength of arm and his faith, the cross began to move, and move, and move, until finally it ripped away from the shield.

A blast of arcane energy propelled him backward. Lux struck the ground hard as the concussive power of the blast knocked everyone aside, including the Eldar God, which now lay in a bloody heap on the square cobbles, its body cut in half by the closing portal. The blinding light was now dissipating, and Lux, through groggy eyes, saw his friend fall to the ground as well.

Fymurip… that's his name.

He remembered it now.

VI

Fymurip wriggled out from beneath the tentacle that was squeezing him, rolled away, and then came up fast and precise, though his body ached from the constriction. He drove the knife into the flopping appendage and twisted the blade until it lay still. He then moved swiftly to free the last goblin that the dying god now held. The little creature shrieked its thanks, then scrambled away into the darkness to meet up with the rest of his friends as they pushed the Teutonic soldiers back from Igor Square.

Catherine lay moaning on a heap of rubble. Her fall had given her a nasty cut on her forehead, though she seemed capable of moving. Their eyes met as he helped her to her feet. He handed her his knife. "Are you okay?" he asked.

She nodded and wiped blood, gore and brick dust from her clothing. "I will be soon enough. Where is Lux?"

Where, indeed? Fymurip searched the rubble near the body of the dead Eldar God, searched the piles of goblin, wolf, and knight bodies strewn everywhere. He turned left, right, but did not see his friend.

That's when he saw the Eldar priest, before him several feet away. The man stood feeble in a ruined robe, but his eyes and face were clean, though touched with clear exhaustion. The man held his hand out, his long, thin fingers pointing in accusation.

"This is not over!" he shouted, his raspy voice stepping over the words. "The Eldar Gods will come home again someday, I swear it. *I swear it!*"

The priest rushed Fymurip, though his body was weak and his legs moved slowly. Fymurip braced to receive the attack, and Catherine beside him did the same.

Out of shadow leapt Lux. The big knight was in near flight as he struck the priest and took him down. Fymurip moved forward and followed them as they tumbled down a pile of rubble. And by the time they stopped falling, the priest's frail body was nothing but a husk, bones broken, face unrecognizable. Lux was in no great shape either, the roll having shredded his tattered clothing. The big man lay there beside the demolished priest, his arms flayed out as if he were mounted on a cross.

Fymurip and Catherine scrambled down the pile. As Fymurip went to Lux and cupped his hand behind the man's wounded head, Catherine took her knife and drove it into the heart of the priest. She held it there for many minutes to ensure that, at last, the old man was dead.

"Speak to me, my friend," Fymurip whispered into Lux's ear. "Show me that you are okay."

Lux opened his eyes, slowly, and gave a small smile. "You owe me a life."

Fymurip smiled back and did not hold back his tears. "I will pay it in spades, my friend."

He hugged Lux's neck, and they took a moment of silence to enjoy each other's company again, until Lux found the strength to stand. Fymurip and Catherine helped him up.

"What happened to the cross?" Fymurip asked.

Lux stood there, seemingly confused by the question. He held up his hand and opened it, and there, in the center of the palm, lay the burned outline of a cross, red and wet. The cross itself was gone.

"I am the Cross of Saint Boniface now."

VII

The armies of Duke Frederick and King Alexander fought throughout the night and into the next morning. At the head of a spear point of Lithuanian and Cossack cavalry, Lux, Fymurip, and Catherine charged the last defensive position of the Teutonic line, but they were unable to break through and capture the Grandmaster before he slipped away to the west of Rostenbork. There was no chance now to finish the matter once and for all. The Eldar priest lay dead in Starybogow, his portal closed, and his treacherous god dead and decaying. But Duke Frederick got away, and as long as Eldar powers continued to hold sway over his actions, the priest was right: the Eldar Gods would, in time, find a way to return.

But for now, the matter was concluded. A balance had been maintained between the Eldar Gods and the Old Gods, and Starybogow remained the center of the struggle that would continue on for generations to come. The only question now was what Lux von Junker would do.

They stood at a crossroads near Swinka. King Alexander had honored them each with new horses, new clothing, armor, and enough food to get them safely back to Germany. But Fymurip could see the hesitation in Lux's eyes.

"You are not going back to Germany? To France?"

Lux shook his head. "No."

"But what of your family? Your wife? Your children?"

Fymurip could see that the question pained Lux, but the stubborn knight kept his emotions in check. "I am not the same man I was but a few weeks ago, Fymurip. The cross is burned indelibly now onto my soul. When I fell to the ground near the portal, I could tell that it was dissolving into my hand, into my skin, and there was nothing that I could do to stop it. And whatever good or evil that it possesses now is inside me. The cross itself may lay in ash in Igor Square, but its essence now courses through my blood. I cannot go back to Germany or France and risk falling into the hands of Duke Frederick again. I cannot bring such a burden onto my family, for as long as I am close to those who would use me to open another portal, I am a risk to all."

Fymurip did not want to ask this next question, but he bit his lip and said, "Will you then kill yourself?"

Lux chuckled and shook his head. "I cannot. I have tried to do so many times in the past few days, but something always stays my hand. Saint Boniface, I'm sure. His cross cannot be destroyed, and thus I cannot be destroyed."

"Where will you go?" Catherine asked.

"To the east," Lux said, "to Cathay, where perhaps there are men who may hold the secret of how I may die in peace and finally rid the world of this burden that I carry." Lux pulled on the reins of his restless horse and asked, "And where will you two go?"

"To Germany," Fymurip answered. "I have promised to escort Catherine back to Lübeck where we will try to explain all this to the League. And then, I-"

"Will you visit my wife, my children," Lux asked, "and try to explain to them why I cannot return? I know it is a burden that I ask, but I trust no one else to do so."

Fymurip considered the request and was about to speak when Catherine put her hand on his arm, and said, "We will gladly see your wife and children and tell them."

"Thank you." Lux turned his horse around and pointed it down the road to the town of Dragu. "Farewell, Fymruip Azat. You are a fine man, for a Tatar."

"And you, my worthy ally. May you always rest your head on peaceful ground."

They bid Lux farewell and watched him disappear up the road and out of sight.

"We will tell his family?" Fymurip gave Catherine a wary eye.

She nodded. "Yes, we will."

"I thought I was taking you back to Germany."

"Not yet," she said. "This matter is not over. Lux may now be the Cross of Saint Boniface, but there are other ways through which the Eldar Gods can enter this world. Avignon, France is not far from Spain. And in Spain, there lays a sword that the League is desperate to find. You are I are going to find it."

Fymurip was about to tell her to kiss his… but the look in her eye, the sweet curve of her lips, kept him quiet. She was beautiful, and despite her youth, she was powerful and exciting. He could turn his horse around right now and leave her here. But in truth, he had no desire to return to Turkey and to Constantinople.

Fymurip huffed and shook his head. "You Christians will be the death of me."

Catherine smiled, gave him a tiny wink, and turned her horse toward Nasti.

Fymurip Azat followed.

APPENDIX ONE

Factions

THE CHURCH

Among the power struggle between the warring god factions, the religion of Christianity is the prevailing faith. The House of God is ever-present in the ongoing events surrounding Starybogow; both factions and their supporters have been branded heretics by the Pope, but there are still those who sympathize with the Slavic people of the old faith, being aligned with the similar purpose of preserving humanity. There are dark murmurs across the land that Pope Alexander the VIth and his highest ranking officials work in the name of God just to cover their own corruption.

TEUTONIC KNIGHTS

The strong-arm of the Church, the Teutonic Knights were founded in the Holy Land along with the Holy Orders. After the bloody massacre of the Knights Templar, they became the preeminent military order of the Church. They cleave across the land with their bloodstained weapons, murdering all that do not serve in the name of God. Once seen as knights of Christianity and having model faith, the Slavic people know the truth; most within the order are minions of the Eldar Gods, which explains their unadulterated, relentless violence. Whether the Church is aware of this connection or they believe it to be superstition created by the heathens, they still support the knights and send them to carry out their will where they need it.

ELDAR GODS

Nicknamed 'the Dwellers of the Deep' and sometimes 'the Dark Ones', these creatures inhabit the Baltic Ocean and thrust their tentacles up from the sea for one purpose – to destroy humanity and replace them with creatures of their own image. They had once been sealed in a Void by Perun in order to protect humanity, but their battle against the Old Gods has been waged for hundreds of years prior. The only people who have truly seen these creatures have fallen sway to their maniacal whims and have lost all sense of their humanity. Those they have wrapped their tentacles around have clear signs – almonding of the eyes, elongated appendages and craniums, and in some intense cases they begin to grow tentacles of their own as a sign of the power bestowed upon them.

SERVITORS

These nightmarish creatures make up the main force of the Eldar Gods that walk the land. As if born from the very depths of the ocean floor, these creatures have the body shape of ordinary men, but they have gained attributes of sea-dwelling creatures such as the carapace of crabs, their garbs decorated with dried-up starfish and cracked shells, their hair resembling seaweed, and the tell-tale look of tentacles granted by the Eldar Gods. Having lost so much of their humanity, they cannot speak the tongue of regular people, but instead their words come out gargled, as if every word was drowned out by water. They travel primarily by water, but when they walk the land, they do in the dark of night, trying to abduct children and convert adults with a trance-like madness.

OLD GODS

These deities of legend are worshiped by the Slavic people and, for the most part, wish to see humanity thrive. These beings come in many shapes, sizes, forms, and varying allegiances. Even though there are deities of great power and reputation, such as Perun and Triglav, many minor creatures fall under this category as well, such as the leshiye, the vampyrs, the topielec, etc. The Slavic people worship the Old Gods with statues and totems, and occasionally there are those cults who perform in the dark rites of sacrifices. The gods do not solely represent power, but some represent the elements and everyday aspects of life such as good harvest and household environment. After having escaped the Void, they live in a variety of areas; some underground in labyrinthine caves and tunnels and many in sacred forest groves.

THE SLAVIC PEOPLE

The majority of people that reside in Central and Eastern Europe in the 1500's; along with the Prus, Lithuanians, Margyars, and Tartars. The Slavs are divided in Czechs, Poles, Ukrainians, Belrus, and Russians, but they all share a common heritage. They struggle to exist in a land where Christianity threatens to overwhelm and destroy those that do not believe. They worship the many different Old Gods, comparable to that of the Greek gods, while Starybogow is similar to that of the Pantheon. In Poland-Lithuania they are led by Alexander Alexander; in the countryside they live primarily in swamps and woodlands where they protect the remnants of their statues and idols.

HANSEATIC LEAGUE

Once thought to be the world's most elite and elaborate trading organization, their greater purpose and most sacred commodity is secrets. Every member of the guild is trained in the art of swordplay and advanced acrobatics so that they can not only trade valuables across the land, but so that they might spy on the different groups around the realm and adventure to the most desolate ruins to find treasure. They swear allegiance to no overarching group, and even though they fight for the preservation of humanity, their main priority is always protecting their interests and needs above the common man.

ROMANI

Mystic free people that roam the land, swearing no allegiance to any group. They do not really care what happens in the war between the Eldar and the Old Gods, but for whatever reason they try to keep the war ongoing; what stake they have in it is a mystery. The allegiance of many cannot be assured because it changes as each side pulls more victories in the ongoing war.

APPENDIX TWO

Bestiary

VUCARI

Once mortal people, vucari have been afflicted with a curse, whether cast upon them or inherited through their bloodline, that forces them to transform into a beast. There have been myths that this is upon the first full moonlight, but there are actually any number of reasons why a vucari's transformation is triggered. The creature that the individual becomes is more wolf than human; the only remaining feature being the ability to stand on two legs if they wish. The degree of humanity loss depends on how advanced the vucari's transformation is. Some transform for only short amounts of time with no control or recognition of human functions; some can change at will and retain full sense of who they once were but perhaps lose the ability to talk; others have fully given in to their bestial side and remain in vucari form permanently but still speak and function as humans would.

BLUD

An ethereal spirit who does not walk on ground but instead seems to levitate or fly. It can completely pass through a human body, and in doing so it causes the target to become extremely disorientated; this can result in complete loss of senses, vomiting, and unconsciousness. It is unknown why the blud spirits are able to do this, but they seem to have some control over their ability, as they tend to work with Slavic people.

DREKAVAC

During a time when Christianity is the prevailing religion, one must wonder what happens to those that do not get baptized. Those bodies become the minions of one of the darker Old Gods and get converted into the spirits known as drekavacs. Usually, a drekevac stays hidden in darkness until it can group up with others of its kind, and then one takes over as the leader of the group, directing the others almost like puppets. Depending on how long the body has decayed before being taken over as a drekavac can have varying results on the appearance. Fresher drekavac have most of their flesh intact and can take on a hideous yet translucent look; yet those that have been decaying for a while can end up being naught more but bones. When they find a target to strike upon, they usually shout to be baptized. There are various ways to dispose of a drekavac, but one of the surest is by holy light, namely from a cross.

DRAUGAR

Those that are dead do not always stay dead. Draugars were once humans of flesh and blood, but have since been reanimated for usually nefarious purposes. They are characterized by their red eyes and inability to feel pain. They usually fight on, even after losing limbs, due to their will to server their master's purpose.

DJINN

A supernatural creature that usually makes its home within a bottle or lamp. Whoever holds the vessel of the djinn is considered the creature's master and does whatever it wishes. Djinns come in a variety of different sub-species, but are always ethereal beings created from magic. Mortal weapons and might cannot usually stand up to the unbridled magical power of a djinn.

EFREET

A powerful creature created from magic. Because it is not from the mortal realm, it can change and morph its shape as it wills. While it mostly appears humanoid, especially when ruthlessly tearing apart its master's enemies, it can become a stream of energy or even a wisp similar to smoke. Efreets are a type of djinn that are associated with the element of fire. They are brutal champions that take up the call of their caller, not being naturally good or evil.

BASTI

Bastis are nightmarish creatures that invade a person's body and then take it over as a new host form. It hides in the person's body, waiting for the right time to strike. When it transforms into its true form, it usually appears green and scaly, with razor sharp teeth and hairy claws. Bastis lurk in the night, when their targets are sleeping, to invade a person's dreaming mind, giving them nightmares until the host body is weak enough to accept the basti in. They are violent and lethally aggressive, but they can be killed by mortal weapons.

APPENDIX THREE

Dramatis Personae

GRANDMASTER FREDERICK VON SACHSEN
The Grandmaster of the Teutonic Knights. He works directly with the Servitors and is one of the most influenced humans by the Eldar Gods. Slowly, his whole beard has been replaced by tentacles, and to conceal it he wears a fake one. Even though he works with the Christians, his main goal is to use the Teutonic Knights to bring the Eldar Gods back to their true power.

ALEXANDER I ALEXANDER
King of Poland and Lithuania, he resides in the latter territory. He does not directly support the Old Gods because he cannot of his position, but he does indirectly through the Slavic people. His army is stronger than the Teutonic Knights and thus after beating them in war, they leave him alone for the most part even though they are enemies.

PERUN
In the Old God hierarchy, certain gods have more power and thus hold command over other gods. The highest and most powerful one is Perun – the god of lightning. He has always seen humanity as being necessary to exist alongside them, and thus fights against the Eldar Gods to preserve them. Even though the war of the gods has gone on for many years, it came to a point where Perun saw the only way to end it was to seal the Eldar Gods away; but in doing so, he ended up sealing the Old Gods away as well. Now, free again from the prison he placed himself in, he looks to reclaim his place in a world that has changed.

BABA YAGA
A witch who has some minor control over the darker spirits but also respects the rule of Perun. When she involves herself in the works of humans, it is usually to sow chaos. Sometimes, she even lets them think they have slain her so that she may slip away for some time. She travels in a house that gets up to move on bird-like legs each night.

APPENDIX FOUR

Concepts

AMBER

Common along the Baltic Coast, this gem has been found to fight the effects of the Eldar Gods and even stunt some of the powers of the darker Old Gods. Because of this, Alexander I Alexander has made sure to hoard the material so that his agents are always protected.

SILVER

While amber might stop some dark powers of the gods, silver can completely destroy a force of spiritual nature. It does not have much effect on the benevolent spirits, and there are those that completely are immune to the silver's destructive powers, but it is the more common and effective way to combat the spirits.

THE VOID

A realm between the living and the dead where no time passes. There is nothing to see and nothing to do in the Void. It is simply the absence of existence where life is imprisoned so that it might not take place in the world of the living. The Void cannot be exited from within, but requires a great amount of magical power from without to free the trapped souls.

ENTHRALLED BY THE ELDARS

Even though the Eldar Gods want to replace humanity, they are not foolish as to the potential that they hold. They send their Servitors out to try and enthrall new warriors to their ranks, and those that do not join perish by the blade. Among their enthralled are the Teutonic Knights, and in particular, Grandmaster Frederick. Signs of enthrallment include almonding of the eyes, elongated hands and head, and tentacles.

FOOLS

Fools, jesters, funny men – whatever they are to be called, they are the key to channeling the powers of the Old Gods. Regular mortals cannot hear the whispers of power from the gods, but the fools, whose minds are clear from all other things, are keen to listen to what the gods ask of them. Because of this, they can channel magic that normal human beings cannot.

THE GREAT
MARTIAN WAR
INVASION
SCOTT H. WASHBURN
City of the Gods
Whispers in the Dark
Edited by Brandon Rospond